THREE YEARS WITH ARES

AMBROSIA R. HARRIS

This is a work of fiction. Names, characters, places, and incidents are the product of the author's imagination or are used fictitiously. Any resemblance to actual events, locales, or persons, living or dead, is coincidental.

Copyright © 2025 by Ambrosia R. Harris. All rights reserved, including the right to reproduce, distribute, or transmit in any form or by any means. For information regarding subsidiary rights, please contact the Publisher.

This work may not be used, copied, stored, or processed in any form by generative AI technologies, large language models, machine learning systems, or datasets without the author's explicit written permission. Unauthorized use of this work in AI training, dataset compilation, or any similar application constitutes a violation of copyright law.

Published by Ambrosia R. Harris

Cover art and design by Ambrosia R. Harris

All rights reserved. No portion of this book may be reproduced in any form without permission from the publisher, except as permitted by U.S. copyright law. For permissions contact:
Authorambrosiarharris@gmail.com

Paperback ISBN 9-798-3326663-9-1
Ebook ISBN

Printed in the United States of America

First Edition November 2025

The Taking of Persephone Series in its entirety is heavily based on the original Greek myths of ancient times. The series takes place between the original Iliad and the Odyssey by Homer. Consequently, the events, discussions, topics, cultures, religions, and the general way of life reflect the beliefs of that time and do not, in any way, represent the author's own beliefs aside from modern Hellenism (religion based in Greek mythology).

CONTENT WARNINGS

Battles
Descriptions of gore and violence
Grooming/Attempted grooming
Child endangerment

BOOKS IN THIS SERIES:

KORE
HADES
DEMETER
THREE YEARS WITH ARES *(NOVELLA)*
WAR AND ROSES *(NOVELLA)*
PERSEPHONE

NOTE

Three Years With Ares is a novella branching off of The Taking of Persephone Series. It takes place during the three years mentioned in Kore (book 1). It is advised to read Three Years with Ares after the first three books of the series but it can be read after finishing book 1 (Kore).

TERMINOLOGY

ITEMS

Amphora – Vessels were used to carry wines and drinks (no lip)
Amphori is Plural

Cella – (or naos) The main chamber of a Greek or Roman Temple, built to house the cult statue

Coffer – Ceilings in Ancient Greek Temples

Chiton – Rectangular piece of linen was draped around the body in many ways.

Kylix – Shallow bowl

Kantharos – Goblet/cup
Kantharoi is Plural

Kline – Bed

Kleidi – Key

Lekythos – Vessel to store oils
Lekythoi is Plural

Oinochoe – Wine jug (lip)

Polis – City-state was the community structure of ancient Greece

Peplos – A long, tubular cloth with the top edge folded down about halfway, so that the top of the tube was now draped below the waist and the bottom of the tube was at the ankle

Skyphos – Bowl

Strigil – Tool used to scrape off dirt and oil during baths

WORDS/PHRASES

Diastrevló – A pervert

Agora – Shops for trading goods.

Bástardos – Bastard

Chairetísmata – Greetings

Enthousiasmos – Intense and eager enjoyment, interest, or approval.

Ergastírio keramikís – Pottery Workshop

Es Kòrakas – Fuck off

Eirini meta ti zoi – Peace

Hetaira – Female Companion "Prostitute"

Ichor – Divine blood, Immortal blood. Has a golden color.

Xenos – Stranger
Kuna – Bitch
Kalimera sta archaia – Good Morning.
Moon – 1 moon cycle / month
Miasma – Stain or pollution. Spiritual contamination
Metrokoites – "Mother-bedder" Motherfucker
Proavlio tis Kolaseos – Limbo
Perimene – Wait
Penemorfi – Beautiful
Syncharitiria – Congratulations
Theamatikos – Spectacular
Theos – Gods
Vasilissa – Queen
Vasilissa Mou – My Queen
Vasilias – King
O Vasiliás Mou – My King

Yperochos – Gorgeous

DAYS OF THE WEEK

Theftera – Monday
Triti – Tuesday
Tetarti – Wednesday
Pemti – Thursday
Paraskevi – Friday
Sabato – Saturday
Kiriaki – Sunday

TYPES OF NYMPHS

Lampades – The torch-bearing nymphs of the Underworld
Naiads – The spring and river nymphs
Hamadryads – The nymphs of the orchard trees and grapevines

CHAPTER I

MENDING ITHOME

The usual tune of the familiar songbirds had been replaced with the gargling noise of Ares's loud snore. Despite camping outside of the thick trunk shelter Demeter had crafted them in Ithome, The infernal drum of his heavy slumber bellowed through the wood as if he were right beside the two goddesses. Kore tugged the feather-stuffed cushion over her ears. Even the hard press of the soft blockade did little to mute the sound.

"Ugh!" She groaned, springing from the cot. When she had offered her assistance in aiding her mother to mend the lands, she'd expected her hours would be filled with early morning lessons and long lectures on the native vegetation. Instead, the past few days had been spent attempting to drown out the grating sound that was Ares's voice.

With light steps, Kore crept over to the small reflective plate. Her curls sat wildly tangled in the tie she attempted to tame them with. A deep crease folded between her brows as she looked over herself. The early morning anger slowly wore off as she attempted to smooth out its noticeable etch across her forehead.

She tried to distract herself by combing out her hair, and when that didn't work, she took the extra time to braid it down. Still, Ares's slumber did not give out and Demeter didn't seem to have the same troubles with it as she slept peacefully in her cot. But, Kore could see the small, white shreds of fabric stuffed in her ears.

An early start to the day would give Kore enough time to distance herself from the camp before Ares woke. It had only been a few days, but the god spent most of his time over her shoulder, making her wildly uncomfortable when it came to her work. The early retreat wouldn't go unnoticed, but the newly sprouting grass blades and shaky tree branches of the fort would inform Demeter of her whereabouts.

Barefoot and ready, the young goddess crept toward the door and slowly cranked it open to peek out to the War God's sleeping sack. With his arms wildly flung above his head and his mouth hung wide open as the jarring noise escaped him, it was fair to say he was a deep sleeper. Kore could only hope it was deep enough for her to creep away.

A noisy lump of a guard. Entirely unnecessary.

Kore tossed one last look to her resting mother before she slipped outside the door. The rubbing wood of the frame creaked as she pushed it close, giving her slight pause before she continued at a slower pace. When she was sure Ares had not stirred, she tiptoed off to the open fields.

Not far from their new home, Kore had been working over a small patch of flowers. Her attempt to pull a few sprouts from the earth as Demeter had requested she do, had all failed. All she had managed to do over the last three days was clone them from a single petal found during her first early morning exploration of the fields. Still, she figured it would be a great surprise for her mother.

If only Kore could just do the simple task of pulling forth

life as Demeter did. That would make everything so much simpler. Maybe it would even keep Demeter from her tendency to, at times, be overly skeptical of the work.

The faint pink petals lifted as she approached, drifting calmly in the breeze in a delightful greeting. With a gentle grin, Kore sat in the patch of newly sprouting wildflowers. The soft press of the velvet petals brushed the tips of her fingers as she greeted them.

"Stronger today than yesterday, I see," she whispered.

The gentle vibrations covered her as the plants spoke to her in a language only she understood. Unlike her mother, who had said the plants spoke words to her, Kore received a different form of communication. Reading their flutters and energetic vibrations, it was not a connection of words but of emotions and feelings. From there, Kore learned to craft their meanings.

The gray sky above slowly brightened as dawn clung to Helios's rise. With the lovely, bright morning came the unfortunate noise of Ares stomping around the camp. Barking questions and orders to Demeter as if he were the one in charge of the harvest's return.

"What time is supper, Demeter?" He grunted loudly enough for Kore to hear, "I have several matters that need my attention for the day."

Heat rushed to Kore's cheeks as her ichor boiled. She could not understand his purpose with them. "What is the need of him being here to *guard* us if he just takes his leave whenever he pleases? It would do us all well if he simply just stayed wherever it was he was going," Kore said to her flowers.

"Are you here to guard us or attend your own personal affairs?" Demeter released a heavy sigh as she got to work on their breakfast. The earth rumbled with his booming laughter. Neglecting to respond with anything more before turning from the goddess to collect his sword and helm.

Kore watched him look over his reflection in the metal headpiece, taking great care to place it over his head. As with his sword, he spoke a few loving words to it before he sheathed it at his side. He tossed a look over his shoulder towards Kore and she immediately snapped her attention back down, not wanting to give him reason to approach her and ruin the lovely start to her day.

She waited a few minutes before peeking up to the camp until she was sure he wasn't coming over. Relief consumed her as she looked at her mother, alone at the fire to prepare the morning bread. No sign of Ares as far as Kore could see, taking the bothersome weight that had clung to her with him. His absence gave her a moment to greet her mother and grab a meal before returning to her work.

Her time with the wildflowers came to a brief pause as she enjoyed her breakfast at Demeter's side. With Ares gone, Demeter wanted to stock up on buns and bread for them to snack on throughout their day, giving Kore a purpose more than summoning flowers.

Before she knew it, her afternoon was spent drifting between the flower patch and kneading dough for her mother. With the last few buns in the fire, Kore took her leave back to the plants where she managed to clone several more vibrant colored sprouts. Many attempts to pull the silly florets from the soil were made, all failed just as instantly.

Instead of the colorful flowers, the deathly vines crept from the earth, twisting and tangling around Kore's fingers in a joyous embrace. She giggled softly as she gently ran her hand over the spiky tendrils. "Hello, my friends," she greeted with a content sigh, "Sorry I have not brought you out more. That blasted god will not leave me be for even a moment. Thankfully he had business to attend today, leaving mother and me free of his badgering."

The prickly spikes twitched. Their sparse, dry leaves fluttered as they spoke to her in their pounding vibrations. A mix of agitation and sympathy resonated between them as they reacted to the frustrations within her.

"He is a nuisance," she mumbled, leaning over the twining vines. Their plot to ensnare the god wasn't entirely bad, though she did not think it wise to display her gifts to such a menace.

"No, no. We cannot do that. Not yet anyway," she sighed again, patting the vines at her side before resting her chin in her free hand.

Of all the Gods for her father to assign as their protector, why Ares? She was most positive he would be of better use aiding the mortals with the current war efforts. He couldn't have been the only option – unless he volunteered himself.

The thought sent a shiver down her spine. Had she known there would have been any sort of guard, she would have put in her own suggestions. "I wonder, if I had requested it, perhaps my father would have allowed Aidoneus to keep watch instead of Ares," she pondered to the vines.

They responded with a twist and curl as their crumpled leaves fluttered about once more. Warmth and curiosity radiated from them, filling her with the questions they sought. Their innocent inquiries tugged at Kore's lips as a small giggle escaped them.

"Truthfully," she began, "I think he finds me rather bothersome. Once I take Mother's place, I will just be another Olympian and I do not think he cares all that much for them."

A faint breeze tugged at her cheeks, carrying with it the near-silent screams and whispers of something unknown. A plaguing sound to which Kore had been subjected to since the first night they had arrived.

Leaning over her vines and flowers, she pressed her hands deep into the soil for support. Determination puckered the skin between her brows as she pressed her ear to the dirt, listening for the source of screams. She was unsure if it was from the war or if her mother had been right in a way about the shades. But she was sure that she was hearing something and that it became amplified with her ear to the earth, echoing in her head as clear as the birds above her.

"Sometimes, when it is quiet. I feel as if I can hear them," she mused softly.

The vines coiled and retracted with a wonder of questions. Another sweet giggle bubbled forth from Kore like a song as she pushed herself up from the soil. It had been a few days since she'd been able to converse with her dear prickly friends. She hadn't the time to inform them of her new and sudden heightened sense.

"No, not Aidoneus, silly. The shades. How Mama said they carry with him. Maybe they are always there. You just have to be silent to hear them," she explained.

The cool breeze shifted to a comforting heat with a hint of cypress and ash. She sucked in a breath and rocked back on her knees to scan the land only to be deeply disappointed by not only the lack of the king she thought was near, but the presence of the god she thought would be gone a bit longer.

Kore dusted off her hands and peplos, taking notice of the holes her vines left as they sunk back into the earth.

"Kore!" Ares boomed, his voice echoing through the open field, "There you are!" He picked up pace as he strutted over.

"Oh no!" She launched forward and muffled the dirt before her with her hands. Filling the holes and hiding the evidence of their existence before he could make it to her. She climbed to her feet, kicking a bit more dirt over the exit holes before facing him.

"Yes?" She asked nonchalantly. Ares had yet to learn about or respect personal space, stepping close enough to her that she had to crane her head back to see him. It was another annoying gesture he pressed upon her.

"Your mother would like your aid with supper. I also have someone I would like you to meet." He gestured back to the camp where her mother and another god stood. The space between them was gaping, but given it was an acquaintance of Ares, Demeter probably did not care for them either.

She looked back to the god with a raised brow, "Oh, alright." And without another word or waiting for a response, Kore took a large step to the right and made her way around the obstacle before her.

Keeping her eyes on her mother, she focused on the distraught look that carved her features and how she gripped the cloth between her hands as if it were a priceless gem. Whatever discussion Demeter and the new god were having, fell silent once Ares and Kore reached the site.

The pale new god looked over Ares with a solemn expression before turning to Kore. She noted the freckles over his cheeks and deep red hair that favored that of Aphrodite while his features likened that of Ares's.

"Kore, this is my son, Phobos. I wanted to introduce you two," Ares said pridefully.

Wonderous, another guard to look after us – or bother us if he is anything like his father. Kore forced a smile as she looked to him. "It is pleasant to meet with you, Phobos," she pushed before racing to her mother's side. "Is he to guard us as well?"

Demeter looked over her with wide eyes, scanning the child as if she were ill or mad. "Are you well, Dear?" Demeter questioned softly. It was not unusual for her mother to question her, that was a nightly ritual. It was the stark look of fright that turned Kore's stomach.

Great, another guard. She shook off her thoughts and forced a simple lie, "A bit thirsty, perhaps." She brushed past her mother to the tree fort to collect a *kantharos* and some water. Passing the men without a second glance and knowing her evening would be even more irritating with Ares and his son.

Having collected her drink, Kore stepped back out to the pit to serve herself some stew and take her spot at her mother's side. Phobos grabbed himself a serving and mindlessly took a seat to Kore's right leaving Ares no space to harass her, which she couldn't complain too harshly about. However, that all depended on how Phobos would act.

Ares grumbled to himself as he poured a *kantharos* full of wine and took his place across the fire. His darkened eyes hard on Phobos. Kore shrugged it off and scooped up a bite of stew, taking notice of the many eyes that clung to her. Her mother, Ares, even Phobos watched her with odd curiosity. She swallowed and cleared her throat, thinking of anything to distract them with.

"This is quite delicious, Mama. What is in it?" She asked

as if she couldn't already tell by the overpowering flavor of dried mushrooms. Demeter looked over at the pile of un-chopped mushrooms with a puzzled expression. But before she could supply Kore a response, Phobos chuckled as he pulled up a spoonful of the sauteed fungus.

"It looks like a mass amount of chanterelles. A fascinating find here, especially in such large amounts," Phobos said with a bright grin.

Before Kore could ask, Demeter responded. "There is not much to gather here. As you may see."

"Yes. I have noticed. But it is coming along. I suppose that is thanks to you," Phobos tilted his head, fixing his gaze back on Kore as he spoke. She nodded and took another bite of stew. Swallowing fully before speaking.

"Most of it is my mother's hand. There is a lot more to mend than I had expected and I can only clone the plants she makes… aside from lavender," she admitted.

"It must be hard work, but with Demeter at your side – I am sure you will do well. Come now, show me what you can do," Phobos urged with a widening smile. He had inched closer but kept a decent space between them.

"Phobos!" Ares barked over the flames.

"Perhaps after supper," Demeter piped before blowing at the steaming stew on her spoon. Kore turned from her mother back to Phobos who was now closer than before. His beaming grin never faded as he waited – disregarding the words of their parents.

A smile tugged at the corner of Kore's lips as she lifted her hand. A rush of warmth fluttered over her skin as a purple haze misted in her palm before presenting a fading lavender plant. Slumped and slightly discolored as it was, Phobos did not seem to notice as his eyes lit up at the weak stem.

"Marvelous," he whispered. Kore held it out to the amused god who took it instantly. The interaction seemed to stun her mother but she didn't seem much interested in ending it. It was more like she feared to put a stop to it. Just another demand placed on her by Zeus if Kore had to guess. "What else can you conjure?" Phobos asked excitedly. Kore lifted a brow, her lips tugging to a smile as she looked over the god.

Perhaps having him around won't be so bad.

CHAPTER II

BARLEY AND WHEAT

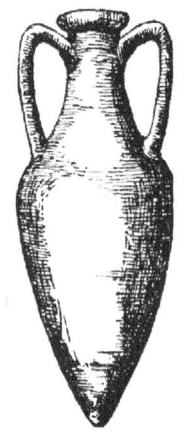

Within a few moons, the cool Spring breeze and sweet air shifted. The skies, lands, and waters grew warm with the oncoming Summer. Which was a good indication that Ithome had taken to their mending well. Fields brightened with lush green grass as the bushes plumped with juicy berries and the trees' branches thickened with the cypress needles. The once silent nights had grown noisy with the creatures of the dark. Hoots of the old gray owl and chirping songs of the tiny crickets created a symphony that rang through the night.

Before Kore knew it, they had packed up Ares's chariot and begun the few days' travel to Thouria to begin their mending there. Unsurprisingly, another one of Zeus's temples sat in ruins, and crumbles of marble and gold lay scattered about the dust-coated paths.

Demeter had decided to make their camp as far from the rubble as possible, knowing mortals would be by it often to begin the process of rebuilding on their end.

The fire kicked up embers and smoke as it crackled with the added wood Demeter tossed in. With the still winds and near silent night, Kore could easily see where the warfront was currently located. Dark smoke filled the air to the south, carried off further from them by the wind, shifting the beautiful mix of setting colors into a blackened cloud of fear and death.

Kore looked off over the leafless trees that surrounded the new battle arena the mortals had clustered around for the past few days. With several tents erected and a seemingly stationary out camp, she was sure they would be there for some time. It became clear, after a few days, that the active camp of soldiers at the shorelines was considered a threat by their very presence. But, aside from them, there had been no sight of any mortals near the ruined temple.

It all filled her chest with a tugging ache. She felt for the innocence and lives lost, but rage also consumed her at the greed of war. Her nails bit into her palm as she fisted her hands and marched around the fortress to the crumbled pile of destroyed marble. The Temple of Zeus was tarnished beyond recognition and left to decay along with the land. How many lands would he have them mend simply to re-erect his temples? Was that all her father cared about?

Of course, it is. He hadn't even enough care to see us off. The words burned in her head as she glared at a stray chunk of marble at her feet. The slow slither of her vines began to wrap around the debris, constricting it as low crackles and pops echoed around her.

"Kore! There you are," Ares's rumbling voice came from the shadows of the trees behind the temple. The vines instantly retreated to the soil, leaving their indentations firmly pressed into the misshapen chunk.

Kore snapped her eyes to the emerging god as he came into view with several wild hares tied to a long string. Pain pressed her cheeks as she looked over the poor creatures, slain to be a meal – not one she cared to eat.

Tucking her hands behind her back, she turned away from him without responding and headed back to the fortress. The sound of Ares's heavy footsteps trailed behind her.

"What were you doing back there?" He pressed. She was sure he hadn't seen the marble or her vines, but she figured standing at the ruined temple was enough to question her. Not that she would entertain him with a truthful answer.

Releasing her anger upon her father's sacred temple would only garner more questions.

"I heard the cries of a small animal," she lied.

"Were you able to retrieve it?" He trotted up to her side, cutting in front of her to block her off.

Kore shook her head.

"Hm, pity. We could have added it to the stew with these." He held up his captures with pride, ignoring the grimace that carved Kore's lips as she sidestepped the presentation.

"Mama will never allow those in the pot," Kore said, covering her nose and mouth with her hands. Once free from him, she ran to their camp to warn Demeter of Ares's plan to spoil their stew with meat. Directing the blades of grass to grapple with his sandals, she hoped it would be sufficient in slowing him down long enough for her to escape.

Heat of the fire caressed her skin as she ducked behind the flames. In her haste, Kore nearly smacked into her mother who was stirring the stew. "Oh, Dear. What are you rushing about for?" Demeter asked as worry began to mold to her features.

Kore took in a deep breath before explaining, "Ares brought a mass of wild hares and he wants to add them to your stew."

Demeter's brows furrowed at the center for a second before falling softer, her eyes drifting to the god as he came into view.

"No, Dear. He will not be adding any meat to our stew. If he wants them, he is more than welcome to craft his own." The sound of iron scraping against iron echoed through the open field as she placed the lid over the pot, her gaze carving into Ares.

"Do not worry, Demeter. I had better plans for this here kill, than that of some mortal grade stew," he scoffed, moving around to his makeshift camp. He tossed the rope of hares onto his trunk and pulled free his dagger. Bile rose in Kore's throat as her stomach churned. Knowing what was to come, she averted her attention back to her mother who was spooning the stew into a small *kylix*.

"Do not pay him mind while you eat, Dear," Demeter whispered softly as she handed Kore her supper.

Kore couldn't fight the grimace that twisted her lips as the faint smell of blood crept up on her. "May I eat in the fort?" she begged her mother.

Demeter's lips pulled down as she gave a faint nod, "I will be with you in a moment."

With no other words spoken, Kore hopped up from the log and headed into the fort. Taking a seat on her cot to eat, her lungs filled with the smell of heavy of cypress, a scent she was more than used to from the meadow. There was a time when she felt sick of it, but now it was a retreat from the stale musk that came from Ares.

With Mama working the fields as she has, it shouldn't be long before we are free of him. She attempted to reassure herself but the unknown time in which the war would continue to rage and the destruction it would proceed to display carved a hopelessness in her chest.

Finally, after several long minutes, Demeter entered their fortress with her own *kylix* of stew. A forced smile carved her lips as she approached Kore.

"How is it, Dear?" She inquired.

Kore hadn't taken the time to taste it since sitting down. She scooped in a spoonful and nodded in approval. There was nothing particularly wrong with her mother's mushroom stew. But after many moons straight, Kore was hoping for something else. Something more filling. "No buns?" Kore pointed as she realized the missing piece.

Demeter sighed with a faint smile, "Oh, Dear. Not this night. I have been putting so much into growing the vegetation, I have not found the time to grow our own stock of barley and wheat."

It wasn't much time or effort for her mother but seeing the amount of power she had been putting into the recovery of Ithome and now Thouria, Kore could see it all weighing on her. She knew she needed to do more. She *could* do more. But cloning plants took a bit more time and Kore was still mastering that. Dropping only a few seconds to clone over the last few moons.

Pulling the life straight from the soil was instant, effortless even, for her mother. Surely there were more ways Kore could assist Demeter, and tending to their own stock of plants and resources was the best she figured she could do alongside her lessons and aid.

"Perhaps I could tend to a small patch for us. It would give you less to focus on," she offered softly. Giving way to a hint of a smile tugging at Demeter's lips. She didn't take her usual amount of time to think it over, clearly exhausted from the labor she was already putting into their work.

"That would be lovely, my Daisy. You have been waking much earlier than I have these last few days. I am proud of your determination to aid the mortals despite Ares trudging along at our side." She ran her fingers through Kore's loose curls, "Keep the crops close and use some clay pots for the trees and bushes. For the wheat and barley – a simple plot of five by eight will be fit for us… Even Ares."

Kore nodded in understanding. It would give her more to do in the early mornings aside from whispering to the flowers about her wishes to have Aidoneus watching over them.

After supper, Kore headed to the back table to prep a pot of soil mix and set out the clippings of wheat and barley they had tucked away for their own personal growth. Once everything was prepared for the morning, Kore took to her cot for the night.

The scratchy and stiff cot was nothing compared to Kore's *kline* back at the cottage. It was another reason she woke right before the sun had a chance to break free of the clouds and just after Selene had totted her moon for the night's end.

After dressing and fixing her hair for the day, she gathered her soil and sprouts, balancing the heap in her arms as she crept from the fort. She managed to grip the branch handle and slowly pulled the door shut. The low crackle of the dying flames and the far-off fading chirp of the crickets welcomed her peacefully.

"You are up early." Ares's grating voice sounded from behind her. It was too bright and clear this early to bother her.

Kore struggled to relax her shoulders as she reluctantly turned toward him, schooling her features to appear as content as she was moments before. "Yes, I offered to aid Mama with our wheat and barley." Ares's face twisted with a quizzical expression as he gazed down at her, waiting for her to finish.

"For the flour," Kore informed. But Ares continued to look puzzled. "The flour for the bread. We cannot have stew without bread." She pressed past him with her arms full of her supplies and her mouth full of choice words she could not share.

Ares followed behind, reaching for a pot to aid her, "You shouldn't carry so much."

"I can manage," she huffed, pulling her goods from his reach to place at the base of the fort where a suitable spot sat. It was on the eastern side of the fort, perfect for collecting the right amount of morning sun. The branches above would make for decent cover during the afternoon as to not scald the delicate plants.

The soil around their camp was the most fertile and lively with them occupying it. It was dark and rich with enough life to support what they would need.

Kore looked over the space to plot out how she would line the sprouts and clones. She did her best to ignore the audience of Ares while he hovered, watching as she worked to move the blades of grass. A slow process, but one her mother would prefer over clearing them out completely.

A little overcrowding along the outskirts of their camp wouldn't hurt. Perhaps the lively blades could aid their sisters in regrowth with the extra push of magic that brewed within them.

Surprisingly and unfortunately, Ares remained the entire process as she crafted and cleared the new bed. "I suppose there is a reason you did not simply clear the space clean," Ares pointed.

Kore dusted her hands and moved for the pot of nutrient-rich soil, "That would be counterintuitive to our work." She scooped up a hand full of dirt and began spreading it about the newly cleared space. Covering it completely with the two large pots she had brought, she was thankful she didn't have to refill another to lug out.

The sun was peeking over the tops of the distant mountains, announcing the true start of the day. Kore was sure Ares would find himself bored of watching her and move on to… whatever it was he did besides pester them.

But there he stood with his arms folded over his chest as his eyes clung to her. She tried to ignore the weighing gaze that dug into her back while she pressed holes into the soil to prep for the sprout clones.

At the end of each row, she attempted to call forth a sprout. She focused her power into the empty hole as she called almost desperately for the seed to appear, for it to sprout and pop up just as her mother's did. But each attempt was met with her usual failure. However, she did well to hide it from Ares, keeping her back to him as she crouched over the dirt.

The energy spilled from her fingertips, racing into the soil as it called for the life underneath. She could feel the pulsating lifeforce as she wrapped her power around it, willing it up to the surface. Her lips pulled up into a bright smile as the soil pushed up in displacement and a sprout worked its way to the surface.

"Come now. That is it," Kore coaxed the sprout with pride. But her excitement was instantly shattered as the tip of her twitching vines poked out. The thin tendril reached for her instantly.

"How is it coming along, my Daisy?" Demeter asked as she came around the fort. "Oh—Ares," she added dryly.

Kore pressed her hand over the hole as she turned to find Ares leaning far over her with his attention on her hand. The pulsing energy of the vine drifted away but Kore remained in her spot as she scanned Ares for any sign that he may have seen her friend. Out of view from him, her hands worked rapidly to replace the hole with a clone sprout.

When his eyes met hers, a taunting grin curved his lips, but he didn't turn from her as he spoke to her mother, "Morning, Demeter."

The goddess pushed past him to get around to her daughter, being sure to move him physically from crowding the girl. Kore took the opportunity to lift her hand from the soil to present a normal—looking barley clone.

"Oh, how lovely, Dear. You already have the sprouts coming along," Demeter mused, clasping her hands over her chest as she looked over her daughter's work, "We will make wonderous bread, I'm sure. When you are finished, clean up and come for breakfast in the fields we last worked."

Demeter turned with a proud smile that instantly fell as her gaze landed on Ares once again. "I assume you will conduct your patrol early, as usual," Demeter added harshly.

Her way of shooing the god off from her daughter. The only other time he was out from hovering over them was the few hours every morning he took to walk the outskirts of the fields where they worked, ensuring the mortals down at the beach hadn't learned of the divine's presence. Though Kore had her suspicions of his true activities, she enjoyed his absence no matter how it came.

Despite the question, Ares remained over Kore as she finished cloning the wheat and barley. She worked with her back to him, ignoring him as best she could while she cleaned the area and dusted the soil from her hands. After splashing them with a bit of water, Kore trailed after her mother, leaving Ares with nothing other than a faint nod of departure.

It wasn't till she was well past the tree fort that she tossed a glance over her shoulder to ensure Ares was not trailing after. When she found the newly crafted garden and the seats around the fire were clear of him, she slowed her speed to a delightfully slow pace to locate her mother.

Off under the cool shade of a high-reaching oak, with roots slithering above and below the earth as it stretched out, Demeter's flame-like hair peeked over the patches of waist-high grass and wildflowers.

Kore thought of it as the heart of the field where they had poured a great deal of their power into the earth. From there it fed the vegetation around its roots and onward in a beautiful chain of life that few could see.

She pressed through the thick, intertwining blades to meet her mother at the base of the sturdy trunk, huddled under a large leaf she had grown straight from the ground. As Kore wondered underneath the far reaching branches, tiny, cool drops rained down on her in a light mist of sweet-smelling sap.

"Is it supposed to be doing that?" she asked with a widening smile. Demeter kept her eyes on the food, shielding it from the rain with the enormous leaf. The corners of her lips kicked up into a smirk, "'Tis not the oak tree, my Daisy. The aphids have returned."

Kore's face twisted into instant horror as she let out a disgusted shriek and dove under the leaf with her mother. She rubbed off the liquid as Demeter's harmonic laugh filled the air. "Do not be such a babe, 'tis only honeydew," she assured through giggles. Kore continued to wipe at her arms and shoulders with a deep scowl.

"Or it is simply bug poop," Kore groaned.

Her mother continued to laugh. "That is why I shielded the food. Perhaps you would like to wash up once again." Demeter pulled a damp cloth from the *amphora* at her side, "The oak told me to bring water and a rag. I did not know why until I arrived. Silly old thing."

Kore gave the tree's uplifted root a playful smack,

"Thank you for the warning as well."

Demeter waited until Kore was well adjusted before handing her the small platter of sliced apricots and figs with a light drizzle of honey. Their *kylix* of ambrosia sat between the two large goblets of nectar. They whispered a small prayer to their plant friends under the foot of the war, pushing their words through the deep-earthed root systems to send the promise of aid soon.

With their pledge sent, Kore scooped up a mouthful of ambrosia and collected her nectar. "What are we to do today, Mama?"

Demeter lifted her chin, tilting her face to the soft beams of light that bled through. "Hm," she hummed with a growing smile, "The oak tells me of a small spring that has just recently flourished after our last energy transfer. I thought you would enjoy filling it with color for me."

Kore's cheeks warmed with excitement at the privilege granted. She had not expected her mother to be so free to her leaving the fields they had come to know over the last few weeks. But she craved the peace of not having a watchful eye over her as she worked. She also missed the spring back at home and her skin screamed for the cool touch of crisp water.

She nodded with a beaming grin, hurrying through her meal before her mother had even finished her serving of ambrosia. The goddess watched her daughter dart about with wide eyes as she took a sip of her nectar.

"Thank you, Mama," Kore cheered as she pressed a kiss to her mother's cheek before joyously skipping from the shelter of the leaf.

"Stay near the spring!" Demeter called after her. The words faintly reached Kore, too elated to be bothered by the aphids and their honeydew droppings or her mother's parting warning, she sped from the field with the guidance of the grass and trees to lead her to the spring in question.

Kore fantasized the relaxing touch of the water against her skin and running through her hair. She felt nothing but dry filth cling to her, and she desperately wanted to rid her hair of the sticky honeydew drops that perched in it.

With help from the thickening bushes and flourishing trees, Kore finally reached the edge of the large spring. She gasped at the sight as she broke through the last of the bushes onto the wide flat water. The crystal clear surface displayed the calm circling fish with such clarity the spring at her meadow would shy from.

It called to her, begged for her to join in the cooling sensation it would offer and she didn't wait another second. She unclasped the pin at her shoulder and removed her peplos, draping it on the low-hanging branches on the shore. With one last glance around the beautiful scene, she dove in.

The bottom of the spring was much deeper than the surface let on. A good few dozen feet below her, and well out of reach for her to stand. But it was the calm she searched for after so many days of work and lessons.

She broke the surface with an audible gasp, flinging her soaked hair over her shoulder as she drifted near the shore where the smoothed rocks weren't so deep. With another pleasant sigh, she relaxed back on a log that dipped into the water. The warming sun danced across her face, arms, and chest while the cooling water lapped at her thighs and stomach. Not a cloud in the sky, least of all the ones grayed by war. Just a clear blue horizon with Helios's burning ball blazing down. It was the simple peace she had craved.

"This was needed," she whispered to the few branches that reached out over the water. Though they were not as cheerful in their response, warning her of Ares's close approach. As they gave their alert, the jarring sound of his voice rattled their leaves, but it was not Kore's name he called for.

"Calypso," His booming voice rippled the surface of the once calm water.

CHAPTER III

THE OCEANID NYMPH IN THOURIA

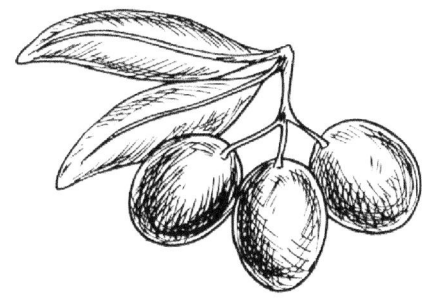

The sound of her high giggles rang off the trees as a small nymph ran into view with a teasing grin. With no time to flee, Kore ducked into the water and tucked herself against the log to hide.

"Oh, Ares. What if Demeter or her daughter catches you? What of Aphrodite?" The nymph giggled and despite her inquisition, Kore felt she did not truly care. Before Ares could respond, Calypso was already set unpinning her shoulder pendent with another giggle that rippled the water's surface.

Ares followed behind, breaking through the tree line. His armor and chiton already partially removed. A low gasp escaped Kore's lips as she pressed herself against the log to hide from the wide-open shoreline she was now trapped on. With no cover and nowhere else to turn to, Kore was stuck for the time.

So this is how he spends his patrol. Kore knew he had not been true to his word but she figured he was just out napping or hunting. He spoke here and there of Aphrodite and how she had been cold to him in recent days. But it was now clear it all did not upset him as much as he let on.

Lust was such a curious thing, though Kore had no experience in it – which may be the reason she felt it so questionable. Most of the tales she had heard that involved it never ended well for either party. No matter if they were divine or mortal. But despite her inquisitions on the matter, she didn't feel Ares best to demonstrate. In fact, she'd rather not bear the memory of such a horrifying act.

With her back pressed firmly against the damp, rough bark, she sought out any form of cover that she could take. But every bit of land from the shore to the edge of the forest was blanketed by pools of sunlight.

The few feet of sand seemed to stretch further than before. She would surely be seen sneaking off. Even so, beckoning the trees for cover would also be hard to ignore. She scanned the clear surface around her. Bright green blades of river grass and deep-rooted willows brushed her legs. She may not have had the plants that resided in the warm soil, but those of the water variety seemed more than happy to assist.

She pushed her energy through the thick wash, reaching deep until the heavy pull of life gripped her. With a flutter of her fingers, sizable bubbles began to break the calm surface. The ripples were quick to spread out from the log, which would only give her away before she could escape.

With a short pause, the ripples slowed while the giggling and laughing continued undisturbed. Kore waited a moment more before returning to her work in a much steadier pace. Though she was still in a hurry, she found drifting the heavy plant toward her stirred less disruption.

After several crawling minutes, a rounded leaf pressed against her leg. Kore tapped the thick plant, feeling the soft padding of the familiar lily. It popped up, breaking the surface with minimal disruption. As Kore admired the water lily, another pushed up past her thigh. Perfect cover for escape, but which way to escape to? Surely they would be useless in shielding her over the shore.

With another glance over the spring and the directions it flowed. Which ways seemed natural for the plants to drift and which would appear strange to those on the shore, assuming their eyes were even out on the water. She couldn't imagine they would be, but who knew? Ares could possibly have a romantic side to him.

Kore dipped her mouth into the water to muffle the giggle she couldn't help but release at the notion. Her attention finally landed on a narrow bend that dipped under an overhanging tree. There were no branches or leaves for cover, but the shade reached out for a boulder across the way. She would need to be quick, but it was the best she had unless she wanted to wait it out.

With her heart pounding against her chest, she stole another peek to ensure they were well distracted. Not only were their eyes off the water but their backs were to her, giving her ample time to skim over to her chance at freedom. Her robes would have to wait and she hoped her mother wouldn't frown at the use of plants for the time being. She did not plan to divulge Ares's antics as she enjoyed the time he was gone and the confession would only bring about conversations Kore would rather avoid.

She took in a deep breath and sunk under the pads. Loose vines under the lily gently wrapped around her wrists while the other clung to her waist. A snug fit against the bottom as they began to drift across the spring with the slow, natural flow of the water. Kore was sure to minimize her movements, resisting the urge to kick her way over to the boulder. She fought to ignore the burn that scratched at her lungs as the stagnant breath begged to be released. The plants had drifted to open water and bubbles would only bring more attention to them.

Kore focused on the new watery world below her, forcing herself from the pain to inspect the stems and leaves of the plants that called the spring home. An entire system of life and death she had not seen before in a wild pond, untouched by her mother. Her spring back at the meadow was made by Demeter with the bottom laid with dozens of smooth round river stones that varied in sizes as they spread the bottom pool to block any life from creeping through.

But why would Mama hide something so lovely and pure? Kore could not see a reason for her mother to hide such beauty, especially with plants. She considered the possibility that her mother may not know. But that idea was just as swiftly removed – her mother was vegetation in all its beauty. It would be impossible for her *not* to know.

Before Kore's mind could fill with the endless line of questions she would have, the pads had drifted over the shallow and narrow end of the spring. The anticipation for air pounded blindingly in her head as she was soon reminded of the burning pain screaming inside her chest. The vines loosened from her wrists and waist as the pads released her onto the sandy shallows.

Her hands pressed deep into the soft soil as she pushed herself up with a silent gasp for air. Her thick hair curtained her as it plastered itself to her face and nose. She gasped out again, flinging her hair over her shoulder before crawling and clawing her way from the waters. The beautiful bolder blocked any sight of her, allowing for a moment to catch her breath and seek a proper escape.

Once her breathing was even and steady, she twisted the remaining water from her curls and looked about the trees and bushes for a likely cover. Nudity was not normally an issue out in the meadow, but in the mortal realm, Kore was unsure of her freedoms in such a sense. With the faint sounds of moans at her back, distracted in their own world, Kore pushed from the boulder and made her way deeper into the coverage of the growing forest.

With her arms outstretched to the draping cordate leaves, the green shades darkening at her touch as they flared out to reach back. Kore released a soft giggle, pulling forth more lively vines to wrap around her, blooming out covering leaves to shield what she assumed were the most notable parts. When she was set with the temporary style, she set out to find a path that would wrap around and land her back at the forest opening she had entered.

Kore kept low, creeping past the bushes that were still gaining their leaves. Leaving her with just enough cover to tiptoe through the shadows cast down by the trees. The sounds of Ares and the nymph slowly faded the further Kore fled, following a low worn path to what she thought would lead her home.

But soon, the calm silence of the trees began to stir as their branches snapped and popped in frustration. The warning was soon followed by the echoing ring of metal blades. Kore ducked low, realizing she had wandered a bit too far from her own camp.

Heeding the warning, Kore twisted her weight to head up the slope she hoped would lead her back to the fields she should be in.

Water continued to cascade down her body, dripping from her hair to soak her feet in mud and make her trek more difficult. With another step onto a smooth face stone, Kore's footing was ripped from her. Her body crashed down into the loose leaves and dirt, sliding over the sticks and jagged rocks that cut her skin as her cover of leaves were torn from her body. The thick trunk of a tree stopped her from stumbling out onto the open beach where mortal men fought.

Ignoring the throbbing in her chest, Kore shot up to scramble under cover. With a wheezing gasp, she peered around the bark onto the beach where war had just sparked. The sands were not yet drenched red with blood but her stomach churned at the sight of a few lifeless bodies that lay scattered across the ground.

She tucked herself into the trunk, keeping close to the shadows of the trees and bush to stay out of view. It would be unwise to be seen by the mortals, more so without her robes to cover her, especially when they were so drunk with blood lust.

Perhaps it would be better to face Ares and his nymph

than to risk the eyes of the mortals. Dry leaves and branches snapped under her feet as she took a step back into a hard body that froze her still. She gulped down a painful breath, ready to unleash her vines.

"Kore?" Ares's rough voice whispered as his hand landed on her right shoulder. Her hands shook frantically as she attempted to cover herself before turning but Ares was already marching forward to view the battle at hand. Unfortunately for Kore, he didn't release her. His grip slid down her arm until locking at her wrist to tow her behind him.

"Ares! Please!" She whispered. Not that her pleas did much for him, she was sure he didn't even care.

Ares stopped just before the clearing where the mortals fought. The screaming of men and ringing of swords spilled across the beach. Kore crouched down, fanning her hair over her chest to give her some sense of cover.

Violence was never something she witnessed nor was it something she wished to view. She turned away from the battle, but it did little to drown out the sound of carnage and, unfortunately, she locked eyes with Ares who was scanning her from head to toe with a hungry gaze and sinister grin. As his eyes slowly climbed up her body, it created a heated trail that left her feeling unsullied and exposed more than she already was.

Not that she allowed much to be seen, she sunk further in on herself to keep shielded. With a deep tug at her lips, she pulled her attention back out to the clash on the beach.

By now, blood soaked the sand a dingy pink shade that washed away with each coming tide. Bodies scattered the ground, some already claimed by Poseidon as they were sucked into the ocean. More screams sounded, some more gargled than others as mortals fell to their fate. The wet sound of metal connected with skin filled Kore's ears in a gurgling echo.

Arrows rained down, shields flew up, and spears of all lengths either cut through the sky or split through the chest of a man. Each pained, ear-shattering scream froze Kore's bones. It was a massacre but with no discerning victor that she could distinguish. She could not even tell who belong to which side. All their metal armor and leather straps were soaked in the same blood they all shed. Confusion mixed with mayhem that only ended more life.

"Look at them go," Ares chortled out as he watched. The words turned Kore's stomach and heated the ichor that had run cold. She most certainly did not want to watch the battle, let alone allow it to continue.

"They will ruin our work before we can even start," Kore objected but Ares scoffed at her words and turned back to the battle.

"We will allow them to find their victor," he offered, more interested in the blood lust and war than in the task Kore and her mother were sent to do. But it wasn't the battle marring their work that she worried about; the victors would need a new shelter after such a fight, a place to aid their wounded and gather rest. They would seek out the nearest place for that, and Kore knew that Thouria would be their first stop before moving on to destroy more of the land.

The screams grew, echoing in her mind with a blinding pressure that begged to be released. She wrapped her arms around her legs, digging her nails deep into the soft skin of her palm.

As Kore turned her attention to Ares, his chipper expression lit her skin on fire. He enjoyed it far too much to put an end to it, and if there was no end to the battle – there was no end to the war. An endless war meant that Kore and her mother's efforts would be for not.

If Arcs was to do nothing but watch, allowing them to continue the destruction that had darkened the land with festering pain and death – then Kore would give them reason to clear their camp.

She looked back to Ares one last time, his attention hard on the men before them. With a deep breath, she called to her vines, urging them up to the surface of the earth between the two sides. The sand was thick and damp, and Kore could feel it move over the vines as if it were moving over her. It was the only thing cooling her skin from the outrage that boiled inside her.

Tremors shook the beach, throwing a few of the men off balance. Sand churned beneath their feet as the vines crept to the surface, their energy seeping over the shore like a fog. It was heavy on Kore's skin but she pushed further. The earth rumbled again, knocking more of the soldiers to the ground.

A shrieking crack tore through the air with a violent quake that sent Ares crashing down. His head smacked against the stone at the tree's base, knocking him out instantly. Kore rocked back, releasing the hold on the vines to brace against the thick tree at her side. She looked out onto the beach where a gaping chasm began to split the length of the space, thick, black tendrils slithered free like hungry snakes ready to feed.

Screaming and shouting continued to flood over the washing waves, but this time, it was terror that ailed them, not the battle cries of war.

Kore stumbled forward, trying to make sense of the sight before her. She shoved her hands into the moist sand to call the vines back. Reaching as far as she could, their energy felt as fluid as water, slipping from her grasp every time she had it in her fingers. She tried again, urging them to listen, but they continued to thrash and grab at the men.

"Come back, come back!" she begged through clenched teeth. Ice filled her hands as she forced more energy into capturing the tendrils.

"What happened?" Ares groaned from beside her. His disoriented gaze landed on Kore, wrist deep in the sand as she struggled to call her vines under control. After a few short moments, his focus snapped with a sense of clarity and he hopped to his feet to look out to the beach.

"What is this?" he barked.

Kore fought the tears that burned against her eyes, refusing to blink and release them. She bit back the sob that clung to her throat as she shook her head with a shrug. The vines continued their thrashing and Kore kept her eyes locked on the thickest most dreadful climber creeping in the sand for unsuspecting soldiers.

Silent and helpless, Kore struggled to make the connection to draw them back. She had exhausted her energy, burned her fingers, and her arms were screaming sore. The sight before her began to darken around the edges as she swayed forward. Everything from the trees to the soldiers spun around her, throwing her further off balance until she collapsed into the sand.

Rough, callous hands gripped her shoulders and gave her a jarring shake. "Kore. Wake up, Kore!" Ares barked from above her. She squeezed her eyes tighter, wishing it was anyone else to have been witness to her stumble.

She allowed her head to roll to the side, cranking open her eyes to the beach where her vines were retreating just as abruptly as they escaped. The sounds of thick groans and gargled cries were few and far between, but it was the eerie silence separating them that stilled her heart.

"Are you alright?" Ares shouted again.

CHAPTER IV

WORD FROM SPARTA

Kore twisted her lips and rolled off Ares's lap into the sand. The sudden blinding light spilled over the blood-soaked earth. Bodies of the dead and injured littered the beach while a reflecting glare bounced off the armor of the bodies bobbing in the water as they were carried out to sea.

As much as she tried to fight it, tried to hold it back, she could not help the sob that broke her lips. She silently gasped for air to avoid the questions. It was only an added blade that cut into her chest. For so long her vines had been at her side, at her command. They had helped her when she needed, protected her from danger and those who would have done her harm. They had always had a consciousness of their own, but never had they gone against her. It was as if these vines weren't even hers or a part of her. They were much bigger and thicker, their color a lot darker than the skinny tendrils that snaked out to wrap around her fingers.

"You do not witness death much, do you?" Ares chuckled nonchalantly from behind her. He dusted his knees off and climbed to his feet with a smug twist to his lips.

Kore swallowed thickly as she kept her eyes on her hands, feeling Ares's gaze crawl over her. Analyzing her in a way she was far more uncomfortable with than his usual staring.

"You will get used to death during your time out here. Slaughter is most common amongst the mortals during war. Whether it be by their own means, or our divine power." His eyes shot over to the spot where the vines had emerged before returning his darkened gaze to Kore. "I do hope to witness *those marvelous vines* again and find their cause ." His eyes dropped as he sized Kore up from head to toe in a way that sent a shiver down her spine.

She wrapped her arms around her chest once more, suddenly remembering that she was completely bare to him. He snickered again and reached behind him to his belted satchel. After a few seconds, he held out a white peplos to her. "I found this by the log at the spring. When I heard the battle begin, I figured you may have wandered off to view it."

"I would never wish to witness such a thing," she snapped, snatching the cloth from him.

"If you say so. I just find it curious." He shrugged.

Kore turned her back to him and fitted the peplos over her, waiting until she had them pinned and in place before turning back. "What is curious?"

"I have been witness to many mortal battles. Both with the presence of other divines and not. Never have I been witness to such a spectacle… Such a massacre. As refreshing as it was, it – well, it leaves me in bewilderment that the very battle you, a new little goddess, are spectating is the very same one to show… peculiarities."

Kore turned to him slowly, narrowing her eyes at his use of words she never would have guessed he would know let alone use properly. "That is vexing." She hadn't meant for her tone to be so heavily coated in sarcasm, but it was already too late.

He lifted a brow with darkening eyes, "Vexing would not even begin to explain it."

"Yes, well. Perhaps we do not let my mother know. She will want to leave and we haven't completed our aid here," Kore said innocently. She knew it was a foolish request that only painted her more guilty than she felt, but she couldn't risk her mother finding out. It wasn't about the vines – if Demeter found out Kore's one time out free to the spring was met with mortal battles and bloodshed, she would never allow Kore from her sight again.

"And why would we not want to inform her?" Ares asked with narrowing eyes, making it clear he highly suspected her to be the cause.

Kore relaxed her shoulders and set her jaw. Demeter had always said a clear voice was clear confidence and though she did not feel it, she needed to appear it. "Because, if she knows a battle took place, she will want to leave. Furthermore, she would not let me roam the spring or further than her watchful eye again. And I worked hard for the privacy."

Ares's gaze crawled over her as his twisted smile grew. "Very well. I will keep this exceptionally important bit of information from your mother. I will just check the decease for any good weapons and we will be on our way before your mother can truly worry."

He stepped out from the shade first, leaving Kore with a hung mouth. He had absolutely no value for human life, and he seemed to take great pleasure from their deaths and wars. Scavenging for weapons as opposed to survivors. Though, Kore knew it was *her* duty to check the men her vines had killed and injured. The least she could give them was an apology before they were collected by Hermes or Thanatos.

Kore took a deep breath and stepped out onto the blood-drenched sand. She was not yet four steps out when the aggressive neighing of several chargers stormed up to her with mortal men cladded in bronze plates. Kore stumbled back with a startled shriek that echoed off the trees. A few chargers reared back at the noise but otherwise maintained their stance before her as the men inspected the sight.

"You there, girl. What is your business so far out here?" he huffed.

"Philoctetes," another interjected in a hushed tone, "Look at her. I don't think she's aware of where *here* is." They looked about the field with confusion.

Kore had yet to see mortal men and she never thought her first encounter would be that of them who crafted war. Though their armor was clean, Kore could still see the faint red tint of discoloration. The blood that marred their soul and spoiled them with sinful miasma. She scrunched her nose to them but remained silent.

She was unsure if they meant her harm but she wasn't willing to take the chance. There wasn't much she knew of mortals other than the tales her mother had shared and most all of them did not seem too kind. But, neither were the tales of the divines she shared. Kore knew they were not much different than the mortals created, which gave her more than enough reason for concern.

"Easy now," the one named Philoctetes said with his palms to her. He removed his bow and sword, tucking them into a flap on his charger's saddle before throwing his leg over and hopping down. Kore shuffled back, falling into the sand.

Several gasps flooded the silent air as the men soon gaped down at the red drenched sand.

"Back away from her!" Ares roared, charging over to them like a great massive bull.

"Ares!" the man shuttered breathlessly before falling to his knees.

"You all are late to the battle. A battle that is far from where it is meant to be," Ares pointed. His voice was rather calm for the intrusion of mortals on the divine worked soil, but it was clear to Kore these were not just any mortals.

Philoctetes looked up to the god before his eyes drifted to Kore, "There is word in Sparta of the divine magic and restoration of Thouria. We came to see of the mender and request their aid to restore Sparta."

"Sparta?" Kore panted out. The only learnings she had of it was through parchments, scrolls, and tales from her mother. One thing she knew for certain from all of it was that Sparta had stone paths. Less fields for her vines to escape if any sort of battle was to show up.

"You came all this way to request aid in Sparta? Of all the lands to require aid. Why would these goddesses aid Sparta?" Ares blurted. The men's eyes popped wide as their attention returned to Kore. She pushed herself to her feet, dusting the sticky sand from her now-stained peplos.

"That is what we are here to do. To help the lands in need," Kore snapped as she shoved at the god's arm, "That is what my mother and I offered to do."

He didn't protest but kept uncomfortably close to her as she neared the kneeling man.

"What damages has Sparta succumbed to?" She asked in a shaky voice, kneeling before the man to be level with him.

He slowly lifted his hands up to his helm and removed it to present the goddess his full attention. His brown shaggy hair was a mess from sweat, dirt, and the stifling, confined space of the helm. It was clear he had spent a great number of days out at war with no reprieve to rest or freshen up as his unkept beard covered half of his face and the majority of his neck. Dirt and flakes of dried blood clung to the wrinkles around his nose and forehead. He wore war proudly, but there was a defeated sense about him.

"Destruction, like all else. Barren lands and dried soil ruined by ash and blood. Nothing grows, the animals have fled, and a famine has taken root. We understand the lands of Greece are riddled with war, and thus far the aid of the Gods has been minimal, but we ask this of you, Daughter of Demeter. Help us."

Kore froze at the title, it wasn't one she was expecting yet it left a painful sting in her chest. She understood most mortals wouldn't know much of her aside from being the daughter of the Goddess of Harvest, but it being her only identifier hurt all the same. Especially, when she wasn't even sure of herself in her mending anymore.

She opened her mouth to speak when Ares's dry chuckle cut her response, "This is a war you mortals must straighten out on your own."

"So we have been told, yet here you are aiding Thouria," Philoctetes pointed with a narrowed gaze.

"Yes, we are bringing back the vegetation of all lands ruined by this war. I will see to it Sparta is next," Kore offered sweetly. She would, of course, have to bring the news to her mother and ensure the plants in Thouria were well on their way to a full recovery before they could even plan to move on. Thankfully, they didn't have any place in particular picked and assumed Zeus would just have Hermes deliver them to whatever land he wanted mended.

Kore couldn't see a reason to wait for his word when there were places begging for aid. Traveling all this way to ensure the request was heard. With a light nod, Kore rose to her feet, holding the man's hands as she pulled him up with her.

"Send word that aid will be on the way soon." She forced a soft smile before stepping away from the group, ignoring Ares as she headed back to the fort to inform her mother. The pounding of the chargers' hooves beat against the earth signaled the men retreat while the heavy footsteps of Ares trailed behind her.

"Zeus will have the final say to that," he muttered, but Kore ignored him as she continued toward the fort.

"Where were you?" He suddenly demanded, "Why were your robes left at the spring and why are you all wet?" His words spilled from his mouth with a slight hint of desperation. It was clear to Kore that he put it together, and he knew that she knew that he was not patrolling the grounds as he said. Which Kore also knew wouldn't go well with Zeus or Demeter considering the battle they witnessed and the men circling her as they did.

"Let us get back to my mother," Kore rushed the words out and headed up the beach path that would take her around to their camp much quicker than trudging the forest again. The entire time her mind spun with questions and concerns on how she would mention the aiding of Sparta to her mother and most importantly how she would continue with her vines.

What if she has lost control of them? What if they were never good? What if they had always held such evil in them? Each step and each question sped her heart a little more.

Once the light of the fire came into view she broke into a near sprint. Ready to be rid of the bloodied sand that clung to her. Her lungs felt as if blades were digging into them but she ignored it all as her foot connected to the plaster path near the camp.

Demeter stood over a makeshift table covered in her pots and sproutlings. A large basket filled with leaves and twigs sat beside it.

Kore raced toward the shelter in a hurry.

"Oh, Kore. You're done in the spring so soon. I thought you would surely spend the day soaking in it," Demeter began, taking notice of her Kore's speed as she raced past.

"Kore, Dear, what is wrong?" Demeter called but Kore did not slow as she headed in for a quick wash. She could hear Ares addressing her mother, giving her pause as she ducked before fully closing the door. She peeked around, catching his eye as he smiled and turned his attention back to Demeter.

"She got a bit of mud under her nails is all," he informed the goddess. Kore was unsure why he would aid her in the lie, but for once, she was thankful for it. She figured the mention of war so close would have her mother marching up to Olympus and demanding their return home before completing the task they elected to do. And though Kore would love to be free of the nonsensical god, and her vines were incredibly out of control, she wanted to help the *innocent* mortals – she *had* to help them.

Kore rinsed the filth from her arms, neck, and legs with a damp rag. Taking extra care in scrubbing her fingers to rid the grime that clung under her nails. She watched as the dirt mixed into the wash bowl, disappearing into it as she wished the feelings that filled her would. Her hands may not have had blood physically over them but she scrubbed them as if they did until they grew raw, red, and sore.

Once finished and cleaned the best she could, she left to dress before stepping back out to face her mother. As she walked from the fort she worked on setting a blank expression upon her face to not give away her new secret.

She heard Ares first, berating Demeter in a low whisper that gave Kore instant pause at the door.

"Come now, Demeter. It is not hard to see you are hiding something within her. You said she couldn't pull life from earth but I have witnessed it for myself a few times," he accused. A heavy rock formed in Kore's chest, locking her heart in an erratic race as it fought to break free from her. He knew. He knew the vines belonged to her and he had seen them every time. The burning pressure of tears pressed against Kore's eyes.

"I haven't an idea of what you speak. My daughter's powers are just as lovely and lively as mine are. She has spent her whole life with me, I am sure if she could conjure such a thing, I would have witnessed it. Perhaps you have only witnessed her power in controlling weeds and twigs as she removes them. She's not fond of your proximity anyhow. It would do you well to keep away from her altogether."

Thankfully Demeter had denied it, but for how long would she do that before she too witnessed the vines?

"Now, now, Demeter – is that a way to speak with your soon–"

"Do you not have a defenseless rodent to murder and feast upon? Go do that and leave me be," Demeter interjected with venomous words. Kore took the brief silence to step out, fixing her features to an indifferent disposition and pretending as if she did not hear a thing. It was one thing for Ares to think anything without substantial proof, besides, nobody would believe his word anyhow. But keeping her mother from finding out has been her life trial and she wasn't about to let some drunken, clumsy god ruin it.

She shot Ares a quick hardened look before turning to her mother with a softened gaze as she stepped to her side.

"Is everything alright, Mama?" she asked kindly.

Demeter pressed her lips together with a gentle smile. Ares clicked his tongue to his cheek and stepped around the table to be in line with Kore. His eyes were hard on her as he sized her up with a suspicious gaze.

"All is well, my Daisy," Demeter answered. Kore looked to Ares, his slick grin still hard on his face but her mother's calming nature told her he did not mention the massacre that just occurred. Clearly, he had mentioned spotting vines, but not the new deadly nature of them.

But why? What would he be gaining for not mentioning it?

All Kore knew for sure was that she wanted to be as far from the beach as possible. "I was thinking;" Kore began, "The plants at the spring were lovely and flourishing and with the grass spreading out as it is, I thought maybe we can continue on to the next village or city in need."

Demeter turned to her young daughter with a look of confusion but waited for her to continue.

"The leaves on the tree gave me the idea and I felt if they were large enough here, it was time we moved on."

Her mother was quiet as she chewed over the story Kore supplied, it was unclear if she believed it or not but her shoulders fell with a heavy sigh. "I do believe we must wait for Zeus's word on our next momentary home. Besides, my Daisy, you just planted the barley and wheat this morning."

"Yes, well, perhaps Ares can request we move. He has informed me that his patrols have become void of violence and filled with color and beauty. I think he prefers a bit more… destruction about him. As for the wheat and barley, we can transport them in your many pots."

Both Demeter and Ares looked to her with shock-filled faces as she continued, "I have always wanted to visit Sparta and thought it would be a wonderful place to aid next."

After several long silent moments, Demeter turned her gaze to Ares, "So long as Sparta is clear of war."

The god nodded slowly in agreeance as he continued to gaze at Kore who held her seemingly innocent smile without fault. She turned to Ares, dropping the grin faintly.

Kore considered how much he may have seen in those small moments of her enjoying her harmless friends. But the thick, deadly ones in the field only likened hers by color. She knew what they were, she could feel them. She had hoped that the distance and her stillness during the attack was enough to sway him from her, but it was clear he suspected it.

She had thought she would gain more freedom to practice with her vines, she needed to more than anything. But not with Ares breathing down her neck at every turn. He hardly gave her a moment's peace before, if he suspected the vines on the beach to be hers, he would be looking out for them more closely.

It caused her pain to doubt the tendrils, she had always trusted their judgment as they aided her through the meadow. She wanted to believe they had done what they did out of the benefit of her and her mother. A war so close to where the divines had been staying could have gone many ways from bad to hostel. Who knew what the mortal men would wish to do with them, perhaps that unknown possibility agitated her vines.

People die at war. Ares had told her many nights during their first moon in Ithome. At the time the words had been grating against her, but now she worried if she was beginning to see his point. To see all the divines' points when it came to lending a hand.

CHAPTER V

A TOUCH OF DARKNESS

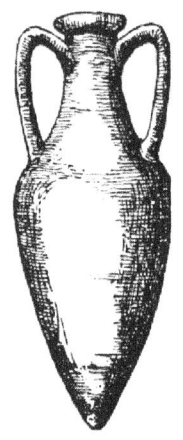

While Ares was in Olympus for approval on the new travel destination, Demeter and Kore took to the fields to ensure the grass and trees were well-adjusted. The sweet, clear air was a welcome sign. While Demeter took to her cypress tree, Kore looked over the bushes and the plants that didn't stretch or reach as high toward the sky. She had avoided her mother since requesting to leave for Sparta, fearing she'd inquire further upon the reasoning for the location. Ares and Kore had kept the meeting of the mortals to themselves, along with the slaughter of soldiers.

Kore figured Ares knew, or at the very least, had his suspicions on her being the cause. Even she knew she wasn't that subtle about the situation. But what she couldn't grasp was why he wasn't doing anything about it.

Perhaps that is why he left so early and has been gone so long. She thought, considering he had left the chariot and chargers to shift there for faster travel. The sun had passed its highest point and was nearing its destination at the other end.

It had been a nagging, painful thought throughout the entire morning. She hardly had the focus to attempt to pull life or clone a single flower. A harsh shiver shook her at the thought of it. What if the vines returned just as thick and full of darkness as before? She couldn't bear it in the face of her mother, in the field so close to her, just a shout away.

She sat at the roots of a thick cypress surrounded by wild berry bushes. Most of her time spent with them was ensuring they were well and ready, but the latter half was spent at their roots, contemplating and discussing the new nightmares that had begun to plague her dreams. Every time she pressed her hands to the soil, the vines beneath her churned and twisted with the same heavy energy.

"I fear if I lose control again, they will do more harm; to the earth, to me… to Mama," Kore whispered truthfully through broken words. The burning press of tears blurred her vision. Twisting and obscuring the shades of brown and green into one big mess. The bushes' leaves fluttered to the left and then the right in response, unspoken words Kore had come to understand over the moons. Their way of speech wasn't much different than the ones at the meadow and it was clear they were not often spoken to by the mortals that passed by.

Their leaves fluttered again, giving Kore hope and encouragement to simply try and clone the lone flower at the base of the tree's stump. A light purple crocus sprung up in the midst of all that had happened. She remembered the tale Hermes had once told her of the plant, but she could not remember what her mother had said it represented.

"Any love of Hermes has to be wonderful," she hummed, brushing her fingers over the soft petals. The purple petal instantly charred over while the delicate pad curled in on itself. Kore snapped her hand over her mouth, watching with wide eyes as the flower continued to crumble to ash.

The sight of the dust settling felt as though somebody had kicked a hole straight through her chest. A heaving pain boiled in the pit of her stomach. Seconds seemed to pass like hours full of silence around her. The only sound to be heard was the thick slosh of ichor racing in her ears.

It was just… silent.

When her lungs cried out for air and her head felt light, she gasped in a ragged, sobbing breath that seemed to cut through the growing silence. She flung herself forward into the decayed crocus powder. Tears poured over her cheeks and blurred her vision as she leaned over, spilling large droplets into the soil. She fussed over the ash that slipped through her fingers, and thin vines lashed out at her angrily, leaving several slashes across the top of her hands and palms. A protest she hadn't the time to contemplate.

She ignored the sting, sucking air through her teeth to tamp down the urge to scream while she continued to frantically work over the plant. Not that she was getting far. Her vision was blurry, her hands were shaky, and she hadn't the slightest clue what to do or what happened. She simply touched the petal with no intent of harming it. Usually, when she wilted her plants, she did so with the desire to, she wanted to. She had control.

Now, like with so much else, she had lost control of this one thing she held dear. Her silent sobs grew in volume, turning from weak whimpers to gasping cries. With a scattered mind, she attempted to collect the ash but each grasp came back empty as it all disintegrated at her touch.

The trees and grass around her remain silent and unmoved. Their leaves lay motionless with not even the breeze to stir them about. They gave no wisdom or words of encouragement. No positive reinforcements or comforts to offer.

She felt alone in the forest where she would otherwise feel secure and surrounded.

She felt alone in her power and placement.

She felt alone because she was alone and there was no one around to offer aid in something they would never understand.

Our emotions affect our work. Her mother's words repeated in her head from a previous lesson long ago.

Kore sniffled and wiped away her tears with her muddied hands. There would be no collecting the remains of the decayed flower and though her mind filled with questions on how to overcome the new hurdle, she decided to pick herself up from the ground. She wouldn't figure it out in the mud, and she certainly wouldn't put a stop to it by wallowing and crying about it.

"Our emotions affect our work," she whispered to herself to allow the words to take hold of her guilt. She lifted her head up to the tree branches with another sniffle. As long as she could convince Demeter to continue to allow her to mend on her own, she would be able to balance her practice and hopefully regain control. She wasn't confident in the plan, but it was all she had to believe that it would work.

It had to work.

She drew in a deep breath, wiping away the remaining tears before turning to head back to camp, nearly ramming into a massive frame. She stopped abruptly, her already panicked heart began thundering against her chest.

"What happened there?" Ares inquired deeply, his gaze on the mess at the base of the tree. A smile ghosted his lips before his eyes danced over Kore's swollen face still damp from tears. "Working against your mother?"

"No," Kore stuttered out. She cleared her throat and tried again, "The flowers here are suffering. I was just trying to see what could be done as they are not taking well to our aid."

Ares cocked a brow up, "How terrible. Perhaps we should inform Demeter, I am positive she would know what to do for them." He turned to head back to the fort.

Kore's heart froze and before she could stop herself, the word had already flown from her mouth. "No!"

Ares paused in his steps before slowly turning back to her with a growing smile.

"I want to mend it on my own. I will never learn if I am

always running to her for every little thing," Kore lied with a sheepish shrug, her attention falling on the new leathers wrapped at his wrist. "You have returned from Olympus early." She attempted to sway the conversation to a new topic, one he would take preference in. One about himself.

He chuckled humorlessly as he followed her gaze to his wrists, "Yes. I had to inform my father of the location adjustments. I also wanted to clarify with him our stance on the war, seeing as how those vines were of divine construction."

Kore stiffened but recovered her indifferent expression effortlessly, "And where is that? Our stance."

Ares narrowed his eyes but the smirk on his lips never softened. He looked over her for a long moment and Kore got the sense he was testing her, if not challenging her altogether.

"He said we are to stay out of it and had issued no aid be given during the battle on the beach. So it would seem it is still a mystery," he finally said.

"Interesting," Kore responded dryly. She attempted to walk around him but he sidestepped to block her.

"It is, as I had said that day. I find a lot of things that happen around you to be… interesting. Lucky for us, my father did hold a bit of interest and concern with the vines and has advised me to keep a much better watch on you. I have already informed your mother that I will be at your side more frequently during your travels around the fields."

Kore's heart sank further than she thought possible but she held her stoic expression.

Finding balance may be much harder than I thought. She wanted to scream but she nodded politely and moved around the god to head back to camp. Waiting only until she had passed him completely before allowing her face to fall and the hard press of worry to carve her features.

CHAPTER VI

THE TRIP TO SPARTA

    "Have you collected everything, my Daisy?" Demeter asked as she lugged her trunk out to Ares's chariot. The chargers stomped their hooves in response but settled as Kore lifted a sliced fig to one of them.
    "There now," she whispered before looking around to her mother, "Yes, Mama." She gave the stallion a few pats on his nose which settled him further. The black chargers were quite possibly the largest ones Kore had ever seen, though she had only ever seen Hermes four. They were much smaller in comparison both in size and mass, where Ares's chargers seemed just as muscular as he was.
    She stood before them with her palm up and another sliced fig presented, feeding the steeds with great delight. She enjoyed the group, though Ares did not often summon them, they were awfully gentle for creatures of war. After feeding a

few figs to the two in front she moved to the next two, supplying a few pats on their neck as she held up the fruit to them.

"That one is Aithon," Ares suddenly said from beside her. The smile she held instantly fell at the reminder of his now constant hovering.

She had to endure not only his presence but his now endless line of questions. Particularly ones involving the sickness Kore had claimed befell the plant she wilted. Each time he toyed at the idea of telling Demeter, which Kore would instantly reject for one reason or another. But if he were to continue following as closely, she didn't think she would be able to keep it up for long. She would run out of excuses soon, especially since she wasn't actually mending anymore.

Kore wasn't too naive to not see Ares suspected much more than he was letting on, and for whatever reason, he was maintaining a sense of silence about it. The more she thought on it, it seemed more dangerous than him outright saying what he knew. If he was keeping it to himself, there had to be a reason and she would figure it out. But for now, she knew she needed to maintain a level of respect. She offered him a soft smile before returning to the chariot where her mother waited.

"It looks as though that is all for us. Are you set?" Demeter panted. Not that there was anywhere for them to sit or stand, the chariot was over-cumbered with their trunks. All except one small spot at the front that would fit one person. That was until Ares came around with a trunk of equal size to fill the space.

"It is a long trail," he huffed as he stepped around to inspect the cluttered chariot.

"Where are we to stand?" Kore blurted as she eyed the cramped space. Ares followed her gaze before a rumble of deep chuckles erupted from him. He snapped his fingers, adding a short bench to the front which would likely fit the three of them.

"It would be best if you sat in the middle to keep you from falling off during the ride," Ares said, offering Kore a twisted smile as he patted the seat of the newly crafted bench.

A sudden sickening feeling gripped her stomach until

bile began burning her throat. She swallowed thickly and glanced to the spot at his side. As much as the idea sickened her, she needed to warm up to him. At least make him believe that. If he felt she was comfortable with him, perhaps he would be more willing to divulge what he knew. At the very least, slip up after a few *amphoras* of wine.

Kore reluctantly took the space between him and her mother. Ares seemed rather pleased with her decision as a smug grin curved his lips. He took the reins in hand and gave them a sharp snap to kick the chargers off, though they kept the same maddeningly slow pace as before.

"Why must we travel this way, again, Mama?" Kore asked, leaning over to her mother and away from Ares.

"Because—"

"My father advises you to view every section of land we travel to ensure your work covers what it must," Ares interjected. Kore curled her lip at his response as she settled back against the chariot and her mother.

"Make yourself comfortable, my Daisy. It is a day's travel to Sparta and we must be vigilant," Demeter informed.

"Why is that? I thought the battles had left these lands."

Demeter looked about the flourishing fields, void of human interaction and destruction for the time. Though it was clear their work had gone a long way in mending the earth, worry still marred her expression as she looked over the lands.

"That is true, my Dear, but civil unrest is everywhere. Among the people with differing opinions on the matter that spread across the lands. The lands we look over are not the only ones to fall victim to these atrocities."

"Now, now, Demeter. Do not be so narrow-minded in these faults. The mortals do what they can – now if my father would allow me to aid them. This would all be over much sooner," Ares interjected.

Demeter glared at the god from the corner of her eyes for a long moment before returning to previous statements, "As I was saying, my Daisy, mortals are unpredictable. Soldiers are not the only ones to bring wars and destruction upon these lands.

We must be sure to make our presence scarce."

Kore nodded and settled back on the hard and uncomfortable bench. "'Tis a long journey then?"

Demeter nodded and Ares gave a halfhearted shrug as he scoffed out, "Less than a day, really." He tossed a smile back at her, or at least, what Kore assumed was a smile. She was unsure if he knew how to smile. A proper and decent smile. One made of pleasant intent. But his always seemed to be laced with darker meanings.

With a quick adjustment, Kore fixed herself to rest her head on her mother's shoulder and her attention out to the land she had called home for the last several moons. The leaves of the passing trees fluttered her way, waving a peaceful goodbye and assuring her the incident with the crocus remains had been well forgiven. She was unable to check on it before they departed, but the blades of grass confirmed the cypress tree was well tending the earth around it with the supplied power of Demeter.

Of course, Kore should have known her mother would supply the trees with such a gift. It was her way of ensuring her work continued in her absence, and she entrusted it with her caring trees wherever she went.

Kore did hope to return again someday, preferably, on brighter reasons. She took pride in knowing the grasses would fill in the dirt patches and the trees would return the shelter to the forest creatures. She knew with all the life that would come, soon mortal men would join in and she could only hope that by then, they would have learned.

Land was precious. A handful of the trees around Kore had been there long before her, long before her mother. And they only continued to grow and watch time pass by with every change in the season. Mortals came and went and did not seem to have much care in their travels at life. A select few made it into the stories her mother shared, and those were the ones that seemed to cherish it.

With a deep inhale, she shoved the anxieties of the flower to the back of her mind to focus on what was next to come. She still had to find time to herself to test her powers when she wasn't so flustered with thoughts of the beach. Seeing how Ares would be with her, she had more than enough time to find out what he was up to. With all of that, she could hardly plan a time to attempt to work with her vines.

Perhaps time in the meadow had made them ignorant to any amount of threat, even if it does not affect me. Kore continued to ponder the possibility that they too needed to learn what life outside the meadow was like. Clearly, they could not discern from one danger to another as a direct assault to Kore, and that would need to be explained. She would just need a moment to do so. She rolled her head back to lean it against one of the stacked trunks to settle in for the long ride ahead.

As the sky turned above them, so did the passing trees as they faded from their growing leaves to barren branches. Draining of life and color the further they traveled from the mended fields of Thouria.

As painful as it was, Kore could not help feel a sense of excitement with what new plants she would undoubtedly come to learn about. The growing beauty of Sparta fascinated her, as she knew it to be one of the most powerful and industrious cities in Laconia. She was sure she had packed a few parchments with descriptions and etchings of the land.

Kore turned to look about the trunks behind her, spotting hers at the bottom, tucked into the far right corner with Ares's trunks piled atop of it. Out of her reach, she had nothing but memories of what the parchments shared.

She knew Sparta to have temples and statues said to be made of gold. Olive tree farms that stretched on as far as the eye could see. Unfortunately, she was well aware that its once-harbored beauty would be marred with devastation. The olive harvest will have long since seen a full season, and will still have a long way before seeing it in full bloom once again.

She only hoped the city wasn't in ruins as Ithome's few temples were. The Temple of Athena had only been described as nothing less than magnificent, and by Athena's might, it should withstand any number of attacks. But still, the limits of the devastation were unknown, and for all she knew, they could be arriving to ashes. A paining thought that only seemed to grow the further they traveled.

The chariot rocked and bounced as the chargers trotted up a dirt path that cut through two decaying mountains. Kore held onto the railing to keep from slipping into Ares, kicking her foot out to hook the lip of the board on the stage of the chariot. Unlike Hermes's outrageously fast rides, holding on seemed much more difficult at the grueling and unsteady speed.

"Are you alright, Dear?" Demeter asked her. Kore tilted her head up to her mother. The chariot bucked and jolted again as the wooden wheels climbed over embedded rocks.

Kore nodded, but a nagging pain pulled at her chest. From the outside, she was able to manage it well, or so she thought. With Ares constantly breathing down her back and the added lessons for mending the lands, Kore hardly had time to release any sort of pent-up grievances she was accumulating over the moons. She missed Lotus and the other nymphs, she missed her spring, she missed the goats and the hens and even the silly deer of the meadow. She missed the freedom she had to disappear into the woods to grow and wilt as she pleased without a care.

But this was her choice, her decision. She asked to aid the mortals and she was granted that request. Leaving the meadow to explore the world around her had been her greatest wish. Sadly, she was coming to learn that sometimes wishes aren't always what one hoped them to be, even for a divine.

Kore spent the rest of the daylight questioning her place and pondering other ways in which she could do more than aid the growth of the plants. She knew their help could only go so far, and mending the harvests wouldn't stop the conflict, it just extended the lives of the innocent. The heart of the issue was the war and that was where the divines' focus *should* have been.

The chariot came to an abrupt halt at the top of a hill that overlooked the remnants of a city. Smoke still smoldered from pockets of ash piled in the streets. Toppled marble and bronze lay scattered around several structures that looked to be temples and homes.

The sight gripped Kore's heart, she sucked in a short gasp before cupping her hands over her mouth. Taking in the horrors that played out not too long before their arrival.

"It looks like we just missed a great battle," Ares chortled before looking down to Kore with a slick grin, "I wonder who the victors were this time. Or who the victors would have been had we arrived during such events."

His enthusiasm for the bloodshed only twisted Kore's stomach all the more. She shot him a dismissive glare from the corner of her eye before returning her gaze to the ruins she would soon call home. For the time being.

The chariot squeaked as the chargers pulled off to continue the path down to the destroyed city. The fading light drew upon the low croaks from the frogs and the soft hooting of owls, with only the chariot rolling over the dusted path to break the otherwise growing silence.

By the time they pulled up to what appeared to be the entrance into the city, the darkness had consumed the sky and no braziers were lit to guide them. The most they had was the small torch Ares fixed to the front of the chariot. The dim light caught and glimmered off two sizable bronze legs. Statues of heroes or gods, Kore was unsure which since they were nothing more than a pair of legs. The rest of the creation had been melted down to a bubbling pile at the hips.

"We walk from here," Ares grunted as he jumped from the chariot. The fire on the torch flickered, cutting the dim light for a moment before casting its illuminance on the stone steps beside them. "I'm sure there is a shelter still standing somewhere in there."

Kore would have assumed if there were any homes still standing, that they would hold survivors. But given the stench of death that sat stagnant around them, she knew that would be a lost hope. Demeter, however, looked to Ares with a sense of disgust and shock.

"Shelter could mean surviving mortals," she pointed warily.

Ares scoffed as he lugged a trunk off the chariot, "Take

a look around, Demeter. There are no surviving mortals. That is why you two are here. The olive tree fields have been destroyed. Just as I suspected."

Kore bit back a laugh, dropping her face to hide the condescending smirk that lit her lips. They wouldn't even be in Sparta if Kore hadn't suggested it first. He had no clue about the trees until he brought the request to Zeus.

Once Ares had collected his few trunks and began lugging them up the steps, Kore and Demeter took to collecting theirs. Lucky Kore thought to pack light when they had first left the meadow. Finding few, if any, trinkets or keepsakes from Ithome, she hadn't grown or added any to her single, medium-sized trunk.

Her mother, on the other hand, had packed one trunk full of clay pots and pouches full of seeds. She also found and collected any plant, leaf, and stem she could get her hands on. In total, she had up to three extremely heavy, and over-sized trunks.

Demeter insisted on keeping Kore mindful and grounded to the plentiful world at their feet. Using what they had without interference from what Demeter called 'magic of luxury'. Instead, she focused all their lessons and studies on the divine power they carried. That did not stop her from using practical magic when tasks extended far past her capabilities. Such as balancing three trunks weighing well over sixty pounds each, in a neat stack that floated behind her as she made her way up the steps.

It was certainly handy when needed, yet Kore could not figure why her mother had kept such powers from her. Even a skill as simple as shifting was left from Kore's lessons. A useful skill, if only she knew how to control it – let alone accomplish it.

Without giving the thoughts much time to corrupt her mind with questions and resentment, Kore followed after her mother, trailing up the several dozen steps until they reached a long-covered court, flanked by the custom marble pillars Kore was so used to seeing. But these had their damages, charred marks, missing chunks, and clear-cut blade marks sliced across them.

The carpet at their feet was slick with blood and oil as the spilled braziers lay scattered along the trail leading to an open yard fit for a decent *agora*. As with the entrance, it was empty with only the chilling signs of a war etched into the stones and marble.

Small, black balls crumbled at their feet with each step, turning to a pile of soot footprints as they moved. The crunching of the odd debris echoed off the silence with a paining tug at Kore's ears. "What are these?" she gasped.

"They are olives. Burned from a great fire," Demeter said with a sorrowful sigh.

"Olives?" Kore repeated as she looked over the dozens of tiny, black balls scattered about the floor and following steps to the next landing. "Why are they all over here?"

"You cannot expect war to be clean, little goddess," Ares said, leading the goddesses further up into the ruins until they came to the crumpled temple of Athena. "We will stay here for the night."

"Ares!" A thunderous voice called from the darkness. Kore looked between the columns, seeing only the shadows cast back at her. But still, the voice raged back.

"My temples have been through enough, without you stomping around!"

CHAPTER VII

THE TEMPLE OF ATHENA

"Do not worry, Athena. I have brought Demeter and her daughter to work the lands and bring your people back," Ares said smugly. Athena twisted her lips into a condescending snark before turning a brighter grin to Demeter and Kore. "Good evening Demeter. Kore, it is lovely to see you once again."

"As it is lovely to see you," Demeter responded eagerly. "Though, I do wish it was on much brighter circumstances. What has become of your temple, Dear?"

They looked around the toppled columns and chunked marble that had been tossed around. Blood splatters stained the once glistening floors. A clear display of brutality and war was left behind, but one thing Kore noticed a great lack of, were mortals.

"Where are the bodies?" Kore interjected as she looked over the stains. A mortal certainly bled out there and met his end, but where was the body?

A memory from years ago flooded her mind as she recounted watching Aidoneus push the boy's mangled corpse into the earth, replacing it with the odd flowers Kore had been unfamiliar with.

Her heart raced with anticipation, but just as soon as it flooded her chest, it was gone once she noticed the severe lack of those ghostly flowers.

With no answer received, she looked up to the three older divines, their expressions ranged from concern to eager enjoyment at her inquisition.

"The mortals have been claimed and given the proper rites by those who cared and were brave enough to travel this way," Athena said warily.

"What of those who were not claimed? What of them? Do they receive obols for the ferryman?" Kore threw out her slew of questions without pause. Curious as to what would come of those left behind. She didn't see Aidoneus supply the boy any coins all those years ago when he had pushed him into the earth. She had thought it odd that the entire being had been sent in such a unique way but considered it the work of Aidoneus's hand.

Demeter's shoulders stilled as she held her breath, her gaze darting from Kore to Athena. Dread slowly crept over her, her cheeks shifting to a glowing gold as the ichor flushed her skin.

"Perhaps we will not dwell on that, my Daisy. Come, let us find a place that is not the ruins of lost and displaced mortals." Demeter pressed her palm against Kore's back to guide her from the temple without allowing a chance for Athena to entertain the questioning any longer.

She shuffled them out into the cool breeze of the night, motionless and silent from the aftermath of war. Smoke still pillowed and fogged the air as the once-burning fire died down to smolder the remainder of the night.

Demeter led Kore to a small field, filled with chard trees and stumps. The grass was littered with charred olives just as the streets had been. But that didn't slow or stop Demeter from crafting another sizable fort from the decaying trees just as she did in Ithome.

This one, however, displayed the evidence of the past destruction and trauma the city had endured. The brittle bark grew with deep charred cracks emitting a light glow from the smoldering flames that still lived within the carnage.

Demeter's shoulders slumped forward once more with a heavy, defeated sigh.

Ares's deep chuckles stirred from behind them, "It would seem this land is less viable than that of Ithome and Thouria, Demeter?"

Kore turned to her mother's fallen face as defeat struck her. The soil was far past ruined and revival would be futile without proper tending, mending, and propagation. The lifeless soil would be no good with the scars left by the fire. The mud was thick with blood, which by now had seeped far enough down that the roots of any new growth would surely fail just as soon as it flourished.

The Goddess of Harvest attempted once more to pull a strong-willed fort from the muddied earth. The ground beneath them rumbled and groaned as it struggled to push out the disfigured lump of wood. Cracked and mangled in on itself, it was a heaping pile of blackened kindling that Kore wouldn't even recommend to a rodent.

Kore's lips curved down as she looked over the mess before them. Knowing it would further upset her mother, she worked to adjust her features before turning back to Demeter.

"It is alright, Mama. We can see if Athena wouldn't mind letting us stay in one of the temples," Kore recommended.

"I do not mind the two of you staying in my main temple, it is the least destroyed." Athena crossed her arms over her chest and looked to Ares with a dry gaze, "So long as Ares minds his trampling around."

The god held up a hand, opening and closing it to mimic

talking as he pretended to mouth Athena's warning. "There isn't much left to destroy."

Athena snapped her head toward him with a deathly glare, "Careful, *Son of Zeus* – lineage only goes so far." She turned back to Kore and Demeter, her grated expression softened to a faint smile, "Please take all the time you need. I have been working to hurry this all along. The destruction has gotten out of hand, yet again."

With a brief glance around them, Demeter gave a hopeless nod, "We will be sure to take great care of it all."

Athena turned to Kore with a stiff turn of her lips, not a smile but not a frown. It was clear Athena had hope, but reservations about the new goddess at Demeter's side. However, it did seem as though she was more partial to Kore's presence than Ares's. She turned from the two goddesses to head from the temple, flicking a disapproving sneer toward him. He scoffed a humorless chuckle before turning his attention to his many trunks.

Demeter took to adding several comforts around the temple. One of which was a simple fire pit at the far end of the *cella* where part of the *coffer* had been dismantled, feeding the flames with a few stray twigs and branches she found lying about the floor.

Kore took to setting out her mother's growing sproutlings along the earth between two sturdy standing columns. She angled them in a way so that the plants would get a few good hours of the morning sun as it rose in the east, and then, as the sun set in the west, a calming golden glow that wouldn't be too harsh on their gentle leaves.

Once the temple was at a reasonable comfort level, Demeter and Kore took to surveying the fields where the olive trees once grew. The strong scent of herbs and floral filled Kore's lungs as she took in a deep breath of the fragrance that closely matched that of honeysuckle and jasmine with a slight hint of oregano and basil. All of which was muddled by the scent of smoke that circled them.

She had recalled the overpowering smell from when she

had first met Athena in Olympus the year prior. It had seemed such a strong and unplaceable scent, but now, it all made perfect sense.

Demeter walked along the first row of charred, dead stumps, and the taller trees less damaged and marred by the flames. More and more charred olives crunched under their feet as they went. A horrid reminder of all the mortals had wasted.

Kore bent down to scoop up a handful of the black, crispy fruits. They practically disintegrated at her touch with only a few managing to hold their form for her to examine. Her fingers curled around the ash as the pressure pushed against her eyes, burning them with tears that begged to be released.

This wasn't just the aftermath of war. This was a calculated attack to ensure the people of Athens and those within its distance had little to no resources. The food had been burned, the waters soiled by the ash and blood. This wasn't war, this was the senseless destruction of the innocent people of Sparta.

"These trees still hold a great amount of water within their trunks. It kept them from burning down completely. We can use the little bit of life within them," Demeter suddenly said with a palm pressed to the lightly cindered trunk. Though its low-hanging branches and leaves had burned away, its trunk was fighting to hold onto the earth.

Kore looked up to her mother with a golden face and drawn brows, "What of the soil?" She looked about the dried dirt, or what she could see of it. The fire most certainly burned away any nutrients they would have needed to help aid the lands.

"We will have to start there, crafting our own mix just as we did back at the meadow for the gardening beds. Do you remember what is needed?"

Kore looked at the ash in her palm and held it up to Demeter with a frown, "There is plenty of ash for the compost to start, and I can search for living soil tomorrow from the outskirts."

Demeter nodded with a small, approving grin, "Perfect. I will join you to grab a bit of foliage that has yet to be destroyed. Hopefully, some seeds can be collected to cultivate the spreading plants."

Just as the wild fruits that grew back at the meadow, untouched by the divine's magic, they needed a few to sprout naturally. Demeter called these *spreading plants* as they helped aid and promote the growth of surrounding vegetation as well as drop their own seeds to carry in the wind and spread. Too much fruit grown by the goddesses' hands would be detrimental to the balance between the mortal and divine.

Kore was never too sure what her mother meant when she explained the balance to her, she only knew that the fruits they grew were used to make the divine's ambrosia and Zeus did not want the mortals to have any sort of access to it. The grass and trees, the bushes and vines all needed their power to return, but when it came to the crops and fields, they had to work as mortals would.

Thankfully the last locations they visited were mostly trees and grass to concern themselves with, but Sparta was a robust city, housing thousands of mortals of all ages. A Colosseum and theater were located near the outskirts along with a number of stone olive press wheels. Egg-shaped tombs were used to store olives while others stored oil, but all had been cracked open to leak and spill all over the place.

Olive fields and barren gardening beds enclosed the city up to the high-reaching mountains and hills that secured it all.

They had spent close to eight moons in Ithome to ensure the success of growth. Kore scanned the land as far as she could see, noting the distance and size of each field. "This will take many moons."

"Hopefully not too long. There are other lands that need our hands touch. Hermes has informed me Athens may possibly be next, though I hear a handful of Hesperides have taken to cleansing and preparing the land. They are doing all they can to aid us when we arrive." Demeter moved to the next tree further down, its bark less burned than the one before but still bald of leaves and its precious fruits.

The faint vibrations and cries came from deep within the trees' roots. With all the destruction and ash, their concerns were muffled, and Kore knew they could use that life force. It was what her mother was searching for, a starting point with a siphon of life no matter how faint.

"Let us move on to the next field and see what must be done there. Several areas seem to be far more affected by the fires than others. We will also want to fetch some water from the stream and see what must be done to cleanse that."

"Yes, Mama," Kore sighed. Already exasperated by the work ahead, but that was what she wanted, that was what she volunteered for. She was out of the meadow as she wished. She was helping her mother, Olympus, and the mortals – just as she agreed. A notion she needed to keep reminding herself of.

Still, she was disheartened by the destruction around her, hoping to have seen some bit of the natural beauty of the world she had been shielded from for so long. Perhaps, the truth of the world was why, Kore could only guess. Her mother never spoke ill of the mortals or their land, she cared dearly for them all. Even during times of war and when they laid waste to Demeter's hard labor.

Kore once hoped to feel that amount of admiration for them. But she found it difficult, at times, to find reason in their disagreements – perhaps that was why her vines lashed out as they did.

Demeter had told Kore of many tales of her time in the mortal villages helping them with the harvest. A job she tended to with great care until she had craved something more, though she never told Kore of what it was.

"Mama?" Kore blurted absently as she followed behind Demeter to the next field.

"Yes, my Daisy?" Demeter hummed back.

"Why did you leave the villages to stay in the meadow?"

Demeter looked down to Kore with a faint smile and brightened cheeks, "I wanted and found something worth more of my attention and care," Demeter gently smoothed her hand down the side of her daughter's cheek, resting her fingers just under Kore's chin, "And what a pleasure you have brought."

Kore's eyes widened and her heart sunk just a bit as the

realization overcame her, "Me? You left the villages for me?"

"You are my greatest creation and I have enjoyed nothing more than watching you shine and grow. You truly have done wonderful things thus far. Hush now, we must stay focused," Demeter cooed as they stepped into the next field, not giving Kore a moment to respond before returning her attention to the land.

She had not anticipated for her to be the reason to pull her mother from her most favored task. She was torn between feeling happy about it but also feeling selfish in a way. Before her, Demeter was free, and now they spent their days barricaded behind thick forests and magic shields. It wasn't much of an exciting life, though Demeter seemed more than pleased with it. Far more than Kore was.

Much smaller than the last, this field looked to be set for cultivating root produce of some sort. Demeter bent down to press her fingers into the dried soil. She removed her dirt-cladded hand and brought it to her nose with a deep inhale, "Garlic."

She rose to her feet, dusting her palms off on her robes. They analyzed the area briefly to take note of the space and previous history before heading back to the temple to start supper. Luckily, Ares seemed to have the same inclination of checking around the city for whatever it was he was looking for, giving them peace while they prepared a delicious leek stew.

CHAPTER VIII

THE UNWANTED GUARD

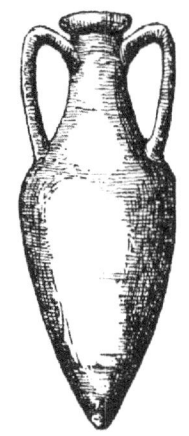

"But Mama! Please!" Kore begged as Demeter plucked stray twigs and stones from the soil she had chosen to work in.

"You are unfamiliar with the lands, and as much as I do not like it, Ares will need to join you. He can haul the soil you find. Do make sure it is free of debris and death. We need lively soil. Out by the trees on the outskirts of the city should do well. You are knowledgeable enough to know what to look for and I trust you." Demeter never looked up from her work, smearing dirt over her forehead as she wiped away the beads of sweat that collected at her brow.

Kore took a deep, steady inhale through her nose, her words collected on her tongue like venom, and her nails dug into her palm. She had thought they would venture out again as they did the night before. Even the lessons would have been preferable over Ares.

    She was sure he was delighted in her mother's approval of his hovering, for once. However, she did not suspect him to drink as much during the day, let alone the morning. But when she looked over to him, she found him selecting an *amphora* of wine to pour into the *kantharos* in his hand.

    "Take the large basket and a few of the sacks. I have requested Ares take an *amphora* to fill with the stream water," Demeter informed. Kore glanced back to her mother before returning her gaze to the god, watching as he emptied out the last of the wine into his *kantharos* and guzzled it down.

    Kore grimaced at the sight with disgust before turning from her mother without another word. She reluctantly marched up to Ares with a hard-carved scowl on her lips.

    "Mama told me you are to accompany me to fetch soil and water," she grumbled as he took down the last of the wine. Thankfully, it wasn't much and definitely not enough to impair him.

    "Ah, yes." He held up the empty *amphora* to her, "I figured you would not be able to carry everything on your own."

    The tension in her shoulders subsided a bit with his words. Despite her reservation about him, she knew there was no way for her to lug the water-filled *amphora* along with soil and whatever else she would be able to collect along the way.

    While he gathered whatever it was he would be needing, Kore collected the basket and a few leather sacks. She was unsure how long they would be out but she knew they may need to travel far to find the best soil. So she packed a few fruits and bread to snack on while they were gone.

    "I am ready," she sighed as she stepped to Ares's side. With the empty *amphora* in hand, he turned with a bright, hopeful grin. "Let's be off then. Hope you are not opposed to walking."

    Well, I am most certainly unlikely to fly.

    Kore shrugged and waited for him to lead the way. He tossed a wave to Demeter who was wrist-deep in the dried soil with a stark expression on her face. "We will be back before supper."

Kore stifled a grumble as he turned and headed off toward the furthest edge of the city where the trees held the most leaves. Not that they hadn't been untouched by the flames, but they didn't char or burn down to nothing, giving her some semblance of hope. Following the liveliest foliage would be the wisest, but Kore was already dreading the idea of traveling so far with the god.

To her delight, Ares was quiet most of the walk, sighing loudly to himself as if he also did not want to be there. Kore considered asking him but felt the question would only open him up to more chatter that she did not want to entertain. She took the peace while she could before he decided to drum up a reason to talk.

By the time they reached the forest's edge, Kore could see that the bark of many trees had been singed near the roots. Making the soil dry and absent of the nutrients she was looking for. Not that the surrounding area fared any better, grass and twigs burnt to a crisp as far as she could see, deep within the forest.

Her shoulders slumped with a deep exhale. With the time for the last harvest nearing and the colder days drawing in on them, Demeter had decided they would spend the time crafting a decent compost to acclimate the plants once their energy wore off. According to Demeter, that would be a few moons after they departed from each location and that meant Kore's days would not only be spent under the watchful eye of her mother but also the crawling gaze of Ares. An uncomfortable feeling that already nagged at her side.

"We will have to go deeper," Ares said with a deep and amused tone. The smell of wine poured from him in a thick haze. Suddenly, it dawned on her, she had only witnessed him take down one serving before they left. That did not mean it was his only one.

Perhaps the amphora was fuller than I had thought.

Thankfully, the trudge for soil wasn't long before the weak trees and near lifeless grass gave hint to a more suitable location not far off from them. Without acknowledging his words, Kore turned in the direction given. The sooner she could gather the soil and water, the sooner she could return to the fort and worry in peace. Given Ares's unbalance, she figured if she walked fast, he would be too busy stumbling about to keep up with her.

Unfortunately, he kept right on her heels with only a slight wobble in his stride. "How do you know how to get around in such a maze of trees when you have never ventured it before?" he huffed. His words were starting to slur but were still well-understood and decently steady.

Kore forced a smile to her lips as she spoke, "The trees and grass told me."

He considered her words but had no further questions. At least, Kore didn't think he did since he remained quiet the entire way to the far-distant and lively soil, found hidden under a mess of fallen trees and branches. A thick pile that took the brunt of the flames, unknowingly protecting the soil beneath it.

Kore got to work tunneling out a few branches, setting aside both the charred sticks and the ones that still held on to a bit of life. They would do well for the compost. There wasn't reason to ask Ares for his help, she figured he'd find his place leaning against a tree while watching her do the brunt of the work. That was expected of him and she didn't mind.

She burrowed deeper until the life pulsated through the earth, calling out for her attention and aid. A thick and heavy birch lay across the needed soil, blocking her access to it. Gripping it tightly, she tugged with little to show for it. Digging her knees into the muck to steady herself she gave another heave, pulling it an inch from its original place. The branches creaked around her, disturbed by the movement of the one holding them up.

The soil under her knees began to churn as the creepy twist of her vines began up her exposed thighs. She jerked her right leg and leaned against the bundle of twigs to hide the tendril she fought to push down and shove back into the soil.

As much as she did need their aid, it wasn't an ideal time

for them to twist around her thighs where Ares could see them.

Kore pulled herself further into the pile, giving a decent shove to the branch that kept her from her prize. The pile groaned but didn't flinch so she shoved again, this time, dislodging the wood from its snare and opening up the damp, rich soil to her.

She reached behind her for the sack to begin filling, shoving as much in as she could manage. The mass of branches creaked again with a slight sway. Dust and dirt began to tickle her nose as it sprinkled down from the loosening twigs above. The pile groaned again with another sway, sending more dust and crumpled dried leaves over her.

Kore pushed back, racing to exit before the entire thing collapsed on her. Something she feared would bring her vines out in defense. Thick hands gripped her waist and with a tug, she was yanked free of the hole as it crumbled to the forest floor. A dark cloud of dust and ash shot into the air around them. When it all cleared, Kore looked up to the faintly inebriated god. His hands lingered at her waist a bit too long for her comfort. She pulled away to grab the sack before shooting him a displeased glance.

"I could have managed on my own," she snipped.

He looked over her with a cocked brow and a curve that clung to his lips but said nothing.

"Let's collect the water and return to my mother for the day." She marched off without waiting for his response, but as always, he kept pace with ease.

"There were snakes slithering about," Ares suddenly said. Kore looked up at him with wide eyes, "One was on your leg, I thought you had felt it."

He had seen her vines, yet again. By now, Kore was beginning to suspect that they wanted to be seen, they wanted her to get caught as punishment for ignoring them as she had. Thankfully, this time, the god's vision was too blurred to see what they truly were.

Kore gnawed at her lip as she thought of an excuse.

"I assumed it to be a bug," she offered after a moment,

stepping around him to make her way to the small pond on the outskirts of the city.

Ares tilted his head to the side with a skeptical gaze. "I am sure." He followed behind her with a few sighs and grunts, though Kore knew his silence was only due to him drumming up more reasons to pester her about his assumptions.

He didn't say or ask anything again until they arrived at the polluted river. The smell of rotten fish hovered in the air. It was clear what was toxic in the waters and Kore didn't need to gather it to inform her mother of what need be done. She didn't even want to stick her hands in the slosh to collect it.

They would have to first clear the water both upstream and downstream before they could even think to find the cause. Kore figured with war, bodies were lying dead in waters, caught up in brush and branches to foul it with their rotting corpses.

The thought twisted Kore's stomach. The corners of her lips pulled down at the sight. "I cannot collect this in this state. We must clean it first." She was speaking more to herself but when she turned around she found herself nose to chest with Ares as he leaned over her.

"Shall we report this to your mother, or do you wish to handle it on your own again?" He asked condescendingly.

Kore held a straight face, ignoring his slight jab about the wilted flower, "Yes, this I would like to inform her of. The river is much too large for me." She pushed the *amphora* into the line of bushes beside the water's edge, scooped up the sack, and march off as soon as the soil was in hand.

After dropping the sacks by the compost pile, Kore had planned to shadow her mother to escape Ares. However, upon their arrival to the temple, Demeter was off working in the orchard fields. Leaving Kore's only retreat to be the bathing chamber. She made her swift escape before Ares trudged into the temple hall. Racing to gather fresh robes to change into, Kore headed for the chamber to wash. Delighted that they now had a space with a decent-sized basin to relax in.

Once her hair was free of dirt and her skin was clear and dried, Kore made her way out of the temple to the fire pit. To her delight, Demeter sat perched on the log, feeding the flames a few dried twigs she collected on her trip out. Kore took her spot alongside her mother, taking in the warmth from both the fire and Demeter.

"Ares tells me your work in finding soil was pleasant," Demeter cooed with a slight hint of disbelief in her tone.

"Uh, yes. It was – enjoyable." Kore looked back to the god, leaning against the column of the temple, his slick smile growing.

"Oh, well, that is wonderful to hear." Understandably, she didn't sound all that pleased with it as she practically forced the words out through clenched teeth.

"As I had mentioned, Demeter, Kore has warmed up to me. Isn't that right, Kore?" Ares kept his attention hard on her as he spoke. She narrowed her eyes with a stiff nod.

"Perhaps, I will show you the Colosseum that is here. It is the only thing left standing after all. Surprisingly undamaged," he offered.

The last thing she wanted to do after such a long day, was spend any more of it with him. She shook her head, ready to answer audibly when Ares tugged her off the log.

"Ares!" Demeter snapped as she jumped to her feet.

"I only plan to share a few words of the city's history, Demeter. Do calm down," he scoffed.

Kore didn't want him tossing out his assumptions in front of Demeter and she didn't want to give him a reason to. She swallowed thickly and nodded to her mother, allowing the god to tow her off.

Demeter watched with fear-stricken eyes but remained bolted in her place as if ordered to remain there. When they were finally out of view of the goddess, Kore shoved Ares's hand off her, putting a decent distance between them as they walked to the Colosseum.

Surprisingly, he was truthful in his words when he said it was the only thing undamaged. She was just unsure of his purpose in showing it to her.

"Ah, as you can see, still standing strong. A marvel to behold, wouldn't you say, Kore?" Ares gushed with a prideful stance. He looked back to her as she approached, still maintaining her distance as she eyed him cautiously, waiting for the inevitable.

"There are a number of wondrous things to behold in Sparta. And snakes of that… nature are not native to this area." He paused for a brief moment before continuing, "Though I would not believe them to be native to any land – as I do not truly believe them to be snakes. However, they did resemble a miniature version of those wonderful creatures we saw on the beach. Now I know you say you hadn't a thing to do with them, but –"

"I saw just as much as you, and I have the same amount of knowledge about them as you do," Kore attempted to lie, but Ares cocked his head to the side with a half-hearted smirk.

"Yes, you have said as much. No matter, you can keep your secrets. I do not care for the *why* as much as I care to know about the *how*." He leaned over her, the foul scent of musk, wine, and sweat seeping off him. "If you do not wish to tell me, that is your right, but I will get to the bottom of these… mysterious vines."

Kore fought back the shiver that raced down her spine, fixing her face to that of indifference. She could feel her cheeks warm as a light golden hue covered them. "Perhaps it was the wrath of Athena or Artemis. It was one of their sacred lands after all," Kore suggested with a slight shuddering breath.

Ares straightened his stance with a lifted brow, considering her words, though Kore felt his suspicions on her were far too great to be misled. He had already been too close for her comfort and now she feared she would never shake him. False sightings of boars would only go so far for her.

She looked to the arena with narrowing thoughts. His discovery wouldn't just affect her. Who knew what Zeus would do to her mother if he thought Demeter had been hiding the power this whole time? What would become of her mother, of Kore if her deathly vines and means to spread death became known by those of Olympus?

Though she was greatly aware it was something she needed to harbor and gain control of, something she was hoping to practice. She had already been distant with them, but she could not risk Ares seeing them again. Especially now that he was set on looking for them.

"What if they come for us next?" Kore said with false fear shaking her voice. The tears that stung her eyes were true but her words tasted a sour lie on her tongue. Ares cocked a brow up as he looked over her. Chewing over her words and what he thought to be true, but he leaned over her with a smile nonetheless.

"Then I suppose my presence with you is all the more needed now, isn't it?" His lips curved up as he looked over her before turning to the arena behind him. "Do you know what the mortals do in colosseums such as this one?" he suddenly asked.

Kore shook her head, though she was well aware of the gladiators and the battles they were forced to fight from her mother's tales. "No," she said dryly.

"Great battles were held here, soon there will be once again. Battles in my name, despite the fact it is Athena the people pray to mostly. The gladiators, though. they all pray to me. For glory, for protection, and aid in battle. It is I they call upon in the city ruled by Athena. Why do you think that is?"

"Because you have an uncontrolled blood lust," Kore muttered under her breath. Ares turned to her with such speed she thought he may have heard her silent words. "I do not," she shot instantly.

"It is because she takes too much time with her planning and contemplating the best course of action rather than just stepping in. She considers a winner and a loser, the benefits that will befall each. In the end, no one receives an answer or aid. But I am much quicker to respond. Giving aid to the strongest and most willed in their pleas. Even the weakest of the pair gets a brief glimpse of my favor."

"How kind of you," Kore said dryly.

"It is, isn't it?" he chuckled brightly, placing a hand on the small of her back. The contact made her skin crawl and she attempted to move from it but Ares hooked her waist to lock her closer to him. "Most think I am simply unkind, being the God of War and all. But I am just as giving and compassionate as Athena ever was. Have you heard what she did to that mortal woman who claimed to weave better than her? Or that gorgon she cursed?"

"She did not curse Medusa. Mama told me she showed her kindness and gave her a gift." Kore interjected.

Ares scoffed at her words with a teasing grin, "That is what she would want everyone to believe. But what kind of existence is it to not lay eyes on the ones you love without turning them to stone for all eternity?"

"No man or god can do her harm. Sounds like a gift to me." Kore shrugged, shuffling away from the god's grasp. Ares glanced at his now empty hand before trailing his attention back to the young goddess.

"If you choose to believe so. Anyhow, that is the reason they prey to me here. Would you be interested in seeing the hidden corridors underneath?" he offered.

Kore fought the grimace she could feel etch her face, shaking her head out to hide it with her hair and answer the question at hand. "No, thank you. I prefer to stay under Helio's bright sun." With one last glance around, she headed off back to the temple where Demeter waited over a building fire.

"As I was saying," Ares blurted as he caught up to her, "Athena takes time to plan, leaving those she deems worthy to live. But those vines. They deemed none of those soldiers fit enough to witness or carry out the tale of what came of them. Only few divines would look at war in such a way – one that doesn't find interest in the mortals."

"I do not have the power to bring life like those... *creatures* – if that is what you are suggesting," Kore lied.

"Oh, but I believe you do Kore. You and you're mother's

attempts to hide it have been mighty clever."

Kore cocked a brow at him. Demeter knew nothing of the vines or Kore's extra power. She was innocent in it all and didn't deserve Ares's harassment.

Fire began to burn in her chest, flooding her mouth with venom. "Leave her out of it," she snapped. She knew she should have composed herself, she should have kept her mouth shut. But she was through with him taunting them. "She knows nothing."

"Oh, but doesn't she?" Ares tried again.

Kore glared at him through narrowed eyes, the heat rising from her chest to her ears, "I do know she knows not of the nymph Calypso you keep having return during your times of 'patrol'. She and Zeus would be so pleased to know that that is how you spend your time."

A deep pinch formed between his brows as his face flushed a dark gold. His shoulders clenched up, his hands fisted. "You dare threaten me?" he spat.

Kore folded her arms over her chest casually, "I do not need to threaten. You seem to think I caused those vines at the beach, you won't take no for an answer. You saw what the vines did to the soldiers I did not know. *That* is what they did to them. I do *not* like you, I do *not* find your company pleasing. *If* what you say is true, what do you think those vines would do to you if you said anything at all? I am sure you found great joy in watching what they did to the mortals. But I cannot imagine you would find the same pleasure if it were you in their coils. But again, that is if what you assume to know is true."

Kore could see the memory playing back in Ares's head as he considered her words. His tensed stance never softened but he nodded in understanding.

Thankfully, Ares didn't have anything to say after that as he chewed over her warning. Leaving the walk back to the temple nice and peacefully silent. She knew it would be supper soon, and she didn't like when he hung over the pot complaining about the lack of meat served. Though Kore was curious as to the taste of some meats he spoke of, she knew it bothered her mother deeply to even think on it.

As they climbed the steps to their temporary home, Kore could see her mother gathering the cooking pot along with the few ingredients they had on hand. She shot a glance of false shock over to the tree line of the forest.

"Oh look!" she exclaimed as she pointed in the direction. Ares released a deep chuckle filled with dark amusement. "Not this time, little goddess. I know you think me some mindless oaf, hunting invisible boars. But I am not as simple as everyone has chosen to believe, trust me when I tell you that. Now let us return, I am starving."

CHAPTER IX

HARDER IN PRACTICE

The sounds of the chirping crickets had yet to still as Kore crept out into the early dawn of the day. The only moment she found she had to try and clone. She had worked well to supply Ares with a few more *kantharoi* of wine over their dinner, against her mother's wishes. But she knew it would leave him incapacitated for most of the morning. At least long enough for her to check her powers. It had been a few days since she last attempted to clone something and a few moons since the Crocus incident.

Now, with the air vengefully chilly and the ground frozen hard beneath her feet, wilting plants didn't seem as detrimental or noticeable. Their time of mending was at a pause but Demeter continued to aid the mortals in other ways. Their olive presses were balanced and the cracks in the stones were sealed. She had gathered as much of the charred olives as she could and sectioned them out into several compost bins, which supplied a decent amount per each pile.

Demeter even took to cleaning out and fixing up the abandoned houses in hopes the families would find peace upon their return. All of this left Kore alone as she would have generally liked it. But of course, Ares was invested in proving himself right about her vines while keeping his thoughts on them tightly sealed from Demeter and apparently, Zeus.

Kore tiptoed from the temple until she was well from view. Though his aggressive snoring rang through the open field, it was annoying when she was trying to sleep, but it made a decent announcement to his waking. With as much wine as he had drank and as late as he stayed up, she was sure to be alone well into the late morning.

The ground was as cold as ice, making her usual barefoot walk less enjoyable. There were many reasons she hated shoes, mostly because they felt odd on her feet, but she couldn't connect with the plants, she couldn't feel them or their vibrations. It felt as if she was cut off from them. Silenced by the thick, muted leather under her feet. It was not as if they even protected her any better with their flimsy soles that molded around the rocks just as her bare feet did. The only thing she tolerated about them was the warmth they provided in the unforgiving winter days. Yet, the silence was equally chilling.

Some of the trees' branches seemed to reach out to her as she neared. Their bare arms gave way to the large gaps between them. Though there was no snow, the brown dirt was lightly dusted with a white frost that emphasized the space between the trunks. They didn't provide much cover as they once did, but it was the best she would find without venturing too far from the temple. When she broke past the first couple of trees, she lined herself up so that the temples fell out of view from her.

The trees did their best in arranging and spreading their branches, but being anchored to the earth, Kore understood there wasn't much they could do. She set her back against the trunk of one thick oak, being sure to face the temples to ensure anyone's unwelcome approach. Once she was comfortable, situated, and sure she was alone, she cupped her hands together to call upon a clone of the crocus.

Searing pain began to ignite her palm. She hissed at the sting, ripping her hand away. Her face fell instantly at the discarded sight. It was hard to tell if it had ever been a flower to begin with. With a grumble, she wiped her hand off on a rag she folded into her robes in order to trap the decay. Whatever it was that was happening to her, she didn't want it spreading by any means.

She rubbed at the raw skin on her palms. The pain would subside, but her powers needed working. If that meant she had to push down the pain and endure, then that's what she planned to do.

Kore took a deep breath and cupped her hands together again. She repeated her process, calling upon a flower she knew well and had never faulted. Lavender.

For a moment a light glow lit her skin, and her energy raced through her fingertips. But just as it all neared a finish and Kore was positive she had crafted her cherished herb, the blazing pain returned to tear at her palms once more. It was more than she had managed thus far, and as upset at the outcome as she was, she held on to the brief moments of power she had felt. All she needed to do was amplify the feeling further. She needed to continue to push herself as she planned.

Above the low whistle of the wind and soft coo of the birds stirring up in their cozy nests, Kore could hear the ragged groan of Ares's snore.

Still asleep. She mused to herself, giving another attempt at a clone. As with the one before it, it lit her palms with a glowing light before crumbling to ash.

Soon the sky turned a grayish-blue, and before she knew it, the sun's light was spilling across the fields and patches of shade scattered the grass from the high clouds that formed.

Clone after clone continued to give her hope just before sizzling away. Each one seemed to last just a bit longer than the one before it. The only silver lining she had to hold onto. A shred at best, but still something more than the fear of never cloning anything again. She needed to look at the positives to keep her emotions from slipping. But even the deepest pains surfaced in some way.

Her vines had not come to her since she shoved them away. Not even to churn the rocks beneath the surface to announce their presence beside her. They had been quiet. Gone.

Perhaps it was for the best during such a time. If she was being honest with herself, she was still not yet ready to face them after the beach. She had thought she was ready to pelt them with questions. But the thought of calling upon them sent a stillness through her that she didn't like.

With a heavy sigh, Kore leaned her head back on the trunk of the tree, exhausted from the early morning work.

The air was filled with the sound of songbirds and the hum of the wind as it blew through the branches, giving way to the quiet absence of the jarring sound she had forgotten to listen for. Her head popped off the trunk as she scanned the gaps before her, seeing only the open field and drifting smoke from her mother's fire at the temple.

Her heart settled, but only for a moment when her peace was obstructed by the heavy crunch of stomping feet coming from beside her.

"Your mother has sent me to inform you we must go gather seeds from the last of the harvest," Ares said as he drifted into view. He held up a small leather pouch Demeter often used to hold seeds and tossed it to Kore as he looked over the space at her feet. His lips fell at the corners before his gaze returned to her face. "Well, come on then."

Kore didn't bother speaking, if Demeter sent him, it would only make it easier for her if Kore complied without a fuss. Even if Demeter had not sent him, he already promised to be at Kore's side for the foreseeable future of their time out of the meadow. She marched forward to the orchard of olive trees where fallen pits had burrowed into the ground and Demeter was positive there were viable ones hidden amongst the tarnish.

They walked to the first field where Kore did most of the

work, searching the dirt on her hands and knees while Ares leaned against a fighting tree.

Dirt clung under her nails, over her hands, and up to her wrists. The earth had frozen over in such a way that it took a bit of digging and clawing to loosen a small section of it. Most of what Kore found were too charred to use and those that were not had been damaged in her attempt to free them of the soil. All the while, Ares huffed and sighed in boredom of his task. Disappointed there were no vines to witness and no flowers to glimpse wilting.

Everything was wilted and even the twigs resembled vines.

"If you are so bored at your post, why not help search for seeds?" Kore grumbled.

"I wouldn't know how to handle them. You look to be having a difficult time with it yourself."

Kore glared up at him through narrowed eyes, holding her tongue from the words she wished to say to him. After a few short, silent moments she returned to clawing and digging.

An hour passed of collecting nothing but dust and dirt, but no seeds. Empty-handed, they headed to the next orchard field. It had taken better to Demeter's hand and was less damaged by flames. It seemed more promising than the last. Again, Kore worked in the dirt while Ares kept to leaning at a distance.

Thankfully the soil wasn't as hard and locating unburned seeds wasn't a rarity, but many were damaged simply from bugs and animals picking at what they could find.

"Would you look at that," Ares suddenly whispered, creeping away from the tree with his eyes set on something behind Kore. She went to turn when he spoke again, "Slowly. Don't scare it off now." He whispered again. Kore turned her head first, moving slowly to see a sizable stag only a few yards off from them.

"Stay here. I haven't seen one of these in moons and I must have him!" Ares crept forward, slowly unsheathing his sword from the leather holder. With another step, a snap echoed across the orchard from a small twig. The stag took off and with a grumble, Ares darted off with it.

Kore didn't want to witness Ares slaughter a deer before her, and she was glad it had fled. It would give him something to do besides hover. He would most likely be gone all afternoon tracking it back to its herd.

Once again, Kore was left alone and had the peace she needed to think.

Kore spent the rest of the afternoon seeking out any viable seeds she could find. As she walked to the temples she tilted her head back, judging the time by Helios's position, finding him nearing his close. Supper time would be soon, and Kore wanted a bit of time with her mother before Ares returned with his defenseless capture.

When she arrived, she found Demeter laboring over a hot pot that sat in the center of a blazing fire. It kicked up and licked at the iron handles, towering over the opening itself but Demeter still worked without a single concern of the flames. She didn't appear to notice Kore's entrance as she stood focused on the stew. After a moment of stirring, she spun on her heels and headed to a small chopping table.

"I have returned," Kore announced as she made her way to her mother's side. Thankfully, Demeter didn't seem to notice, or maybe she just did not care for where Ares was, allowing her and her mother to prepare the supper. Kore took to chopping up ginger roots and garlic, to plop into the cooking pot before moving to the next item Demeter had lined up.

"Kore?" she called from across the fire pit.

Kore continued her chopping as she looked over the flames.

"Where is Ares?" Demeter began, looking around the godless temple for the one in question, "Please do not tell me you sent him on one of those wild boar hunts again."

A twisted smile curved Kore's lips, "Alright. I will not." A small giggle escaped her as she returned to the chopping. Though, this time she had not sent him away by her false claims, he was off hunting again. Perhaps not a boar, but Kore did not find that it mattered in the end. He was gone for the time.

"Kore!" Demeter whined, "Do you not think he will learn of your tricks one day?"

It had never been a worry on Kore's mind as the god always managed to find something during his outings. "It is not as if he comes back empty-handed. He always finds some creature to feast upon." She paused with a heavy sigh before continuing, "Besides, if he has not figured it out by now, I do not think he ever will. Is the break not peaceful?" She scooped up a handful of mushrooms and carried them to the pot.

Demeter eyed her with a soft smile, "It has been. I only worry he will not take it well once he finds out."

Kore dropped the mushrooms into the pot with another mischievous chuckle. Though she was certain by his words before, he had clearly realized her tricks to rid them of him, but he'd leave nonetheless, perhaps to visit with the nymphs some more. But that was just another secret she and the God of War were keeping.

"*If* he finds out," she teased.

Demeter looked to her daughter with a blank gaze for a moment before her lips curved up in amusement, "*If?* If is well enough, I suppose. Go clean yourself up for supper."

With the stew boiling and nothing left to chop, Kore excused herself to the bathing chamber to rid the dirt from her hair and skin.

But she found the empty silence of being alone with nothing to busy herself, left her with endless time to sit within her own mind where her worries and troubles echoed louder and louder. Even with the faintest hint of progress, she felt restless over it. She couldn't find the connection between her ability to clone and her vines. She had always figured them to be separate, just as her powers were.

But what if they aren't separate? She thought over the

possibility that her vines may have more control than she could even fathom. And that was a harrowing thought that stilled her chest and filled her mind with more to worry on during her bath.

Once the water dropped to an unbearably cold temperature, she exited and dried out her hair in a somber haze, combing it out and braiding it down as she always did. The smell of cooked mushrooms poured in from the open temple but she decided to steady her mind with a spinning wheel she had found in one of the abandoned homes.

She hummed a tune she and Lotus had made when they were young, one Kore would hum at the edge of the pond. Though Kore never intended the song to be a calling, Lotus knew to come right away and comfort her dear friend. Only this time there was no pond to catch her tears and no Lotus to wipe them away.

Tears pressed against her eyes with a sting, but before they had the chance to roll down her warm cheeks, the door to her chamber creaked open to present her mother. The hum continued to flow to hold her together as Demeter stepped to the back of the chamber to place the *kylixi* of stew down. She managed to tuck the tears away… for the moment so there was no questioning on what brought them on and no need to lie about it.

"That smells wonderful, Mama," Kore said in a cheery tune, though she could hear the slight crack of her voice at the end. She winced at it but her mother didn't seem to notice as she took several deep breaths.

"Thank you, my Daisy. Sit, I have a few words to share with you." Demeter gestured to the stools alongside her, pulling Kore's out for her before seating herself. Kore noticed her mother's hands twist at the fabric in her lap, a nervous habit Kore had not seen in a long while. Her heart sank as she looked up to meet her mother's concern-filled eyes.

"What is it, Mama?" She pressed, but deep down, she had a feeling she already knew what was coming.

"It would seem we have a meeting with Zeus tomorrow," Demeter said through a heavy sigh.

"On Olympus? Will he be allowing us to return home?" Kore asked with false hope, the look in her mother's eyes told her there would be no returning home. Not anytime soon, anyway.

"I fear not. It would seem we will be with Ares just a bit longer." The words sank Kore's heart more than she was prepared for. Perhaps it was the mention of Ares having to be with them, but she had known he would be. Of course, he would be.

Her vines put her mother in danger just as much as they had her. She scrunched her nose at the news and fought the creeping tears that squeezed their way into her vision.

"If that is all the horrid news to be given, why must we travel all the way up there?" Another concern that began to torment her mind. What if Ares's suspicions found their way to Zeus and it was questions her father had for her? Perhaps it wasn't even Ares to inform him.

It was a large number of deaths after all, maybe it was Thanatos? Maybe Hermes. Maybe even Aidoneus. Her heart sank again – what would he think of her if he found out she had vines in her control that would cause such an uprise in shades to his realm?

Demeter shifted uncomfortably, her hands tightening in the fabric at her lap, "I suppose to hear of our next destination. But I plan to request our return home." She immediately turned to take a spoonful of stew as if to avoid saying more.

"Father will never allow it," Kore said mindlessly, her thoughts climbing over the lost reasons they had to return home. If anything, Kore's vines made it so their return would be a lengthy one.

She took a bite of the stew, knowing that if not her, then the mortals, and if not the mortals, then the divines themselves.

"The war will end soon, my Daisy," Demeter attempted to consol but Kore felt nothing.

She glanced up at her mother, feeling as though if anyone would understand, it would be her. "The wars will end when the last mortal has fallen. No sooner than that." She wasn't sure where the thought had come from, nor had she meant to speak it aloud. But Kore watched the fear creep on Demeter's face, before dropping her head back to her supper.

Kore was first to step off the Chariot once the chargers were pulled to a steady stop. Not that it mattered, the brash god was at her side just as swiftly, wrapping his arm around her shoulders once again. She fought the full body shiver as the creeping feeling clawed over her skin.

Demeter stepped off the chariot in a huff, ready to protest when Ares held his free hand up to stop her, "Demeter, you go ahead and meet with my father in the council chamber. I'll escort Kore." He pulled her into his side, the uncomfortable feeling of his touch felt heavier than his usual general annoyances on her skin. It was more threatening and demanding of her time.

"I think I will walk with my mother. Thank you." She shimmied from under his grasp, making her escape to her mother when his thick hand chained her wrist again.

Demeter reached for her a second time, and Ares tugged Kore behind him so that all she saw was her mother's frightened, yet severely annoyed expression. Kore was unsure what look he had given her but she didn't want to push the situation any further.

"Very well," Demeter whispered defeatedly.

"It is alright, Mama," Kore assured.

"See, it will be alright, Demeter," Ares repeated with a tightening grip. The Goddess of Harvest glared at him with vengeful eyes before she reluctantly turned and headed off while Ares seemed to wait until she was out of sight before speaking again.

"You know, my father states there was no divine aid on his part or that of anyone on Olympus, and he is increasingly curious – as am I – about the cause of the near three-hundred men slaughtered. A number that seemed to go unnoticed by even the King of the Underworld somehow. At least, that is how my father puts it. Perhaps Hades does not care the number of shades spilling in, but my father does," the god prattled.

"Perhaps you should have looked over the field more, perhaps there is a protection placed on the grounds. Have you interrogated Athena?" Kore attempted to skew the god's assumptions. But he only gave a deep, unimpressed chuckle.

"I do not think further investigations would be needed on that beach. I did, however, warn my father of the battles that are circling around. He and my mother expressed concern over the newly mended lands and how well they would withstand a second round of battle." He guided Kore into the palace, toward the Council Hall. Taking each step painstakingly slow to keep her within his grasp.

The only moment of retreat from the crawling feeling came when they reached the garden. Where the flowers and herbs reached out to her happily with provided comfort. Though it was a short pause from the man at her side, it was a welcome feeling she needed.

Her mother's voice flowed from above, raw and thick with despair. "Yes, but my daughter and I are aiding them. Are we not? And now we must return to do it once again. Then what? What if they destroy that harvest as well? I can only mend so much, and I fear this will be far too much on a young divine just gaining control of her powers."

The sound around her fell to an immediate silence. Even the gardens halted their vibrations of joy as the air fell cold around her. The only sound she could hear was the steady beat of her heart as it echoed off the marble.

Zeus's booming voice settled but Kore was too distracted to have heard what more he wanted of them. It was Hera's soft tone that caught her attention away from counting the beats that rattled her chest.

"Please, sister. The mortals of the villages are begging us. We cannot leave them without. You and Kore have done wonders. We ask that you do it once more. Just a few more moons."

The chamber fell silent as Zeus's gaze fell to Kore and Ares entering together, a bright smile pulling at his lips as if the sight pleased him, "Ares, you will continue to join them." With a brief pause, he cleared his throat and added, "For their protection."

Ares's arm tightened around her shoulder, filling her mind with the foul annoyance she was bound to endure for who knew how much longer. "At your request," he chortled.

"Was there anything else you needed of us?" Demeter interjected abruptly.

Zeus leaned back on his throne, rubbing his hand over his beard as he spoke, "No, that is all. Hera thought it would be best to give the news in person."

Hera stepped from her golden throne to embrace Demeter, whispering a few words into the goddess's ear. After several long moments, they separated with Demeter offering a soft bow before turning and marching toward Kore. Her arm locked with her daughter's as she towed her from the god and chamber with haste. Surprisingly, Ares released her to step into the chamber with the king and queen.

Kore shot a glance back, fear chilling the ichor in her veins as she considered the reasons he would linger. He said himself he had already presented the spectacle of the vines to their father, what more would he need to stay and discuss?

She swallowed against the lump that began to form in her throat. "I do not wish to be with him in the fields longer!" Kore huffed.

Demeter continued to hurry her down the steps to the chariot. Speaking her sorrowful words as she clung to the girl, "I know, Dear. I know. But we must."

CHAPTER X

BACK IN THOURIA

"Come, we must leave now before Ares claims we are moving too slow."

Kore hopped to her feet and followed her mother to the bench Ares had constructed on the front for their travels. It wasn't long before the god stepped around to load the last of his weapons onto the back and climb on himself. He gave Kore a crawling smile and flicked the reigns against the chargers.

An echoing groan sounded from the wooden wheels as the chariot began forward. Hitting every rock on the way to make for a less-than-enjoyable ride once again. She had hoped the need to focus on staying in her spot and not being thrown free from the cart would keep her mind busy enough. Yet all that plagued her were thoughts of her vines, her cloning abilities, and the crocus back in Thouria.

As much as she tried to fight it, to avoid another emotionally driven massacre, the feeling of failure continued to carve into her chest. Burrowing deeper with the passing time and again, she felt as though everything was moving too slowly despite the blanket of orange and pink spreading across the sky.

"You have been quiet, my Daisy. What fills you with such worry?" Demeter suddenly cooed from above. Her hand fell into Kore's loose curls to gingerly comb through the top. The chariot rocked as it hit another jutting rock in the path, slamming Kore against Ares's side.

"Just the uncomfortable travel, Mama," Kore lied as she tried to situate herself back in her place. Demeter's hand slid down to Kore's cheek as she looked over her daughter with an encouraging curve to her lips.

"Only a bit longer, my Love."

When they arrived back in Thouria, Kore wouldn't say it was as bad as their first visit, but still, war had returned. At least, it looked to have been war. There was one difference between this time and the last. A screaming discrepancy that chewed into her side.

"Hm, someone must have collected the dead already," Demeter whispered to herself as she exited the chariot. A mindless assumption Kore hoped was true.

Ares looked around their old camp, the remnants of which had long since disappeared. With their attention off her, Kore inched toward the direction she knew the tree to be. She pushed down the aching feeling that had gripped her that morning. It wasn't hard to see her emotions were greatly affecting her work. More so than it had before. She was beginning to realize that keeping her mind from sorrowing thoughts was the best route.

She took another step, trying to allow the calm to wash over her.

"Kore, my Daisy." Demeter called to her, "Please stay near. 'Tis too dark for any proper inspections."

"Oh, I was just going to see –"

"Please, Kore." Demeter's voice was stern and demanding. It wasn't often she used that tone of voice with her daughter but when she did, Kore understood there was nothing more to be said. Though, she had not been prepared for it to be used so swiftly.

Kore hesitantly nodded, taken aback by the sudden hostility in her mother. Demeter's eyes danced between Kore and the dark trail before shooting to Ares. When she was sure he was busy with his trunks, she turned back to her daughter with a contorted look of concern and fear.

The young goddess nodded in understanding. He had been invading their space well enough as it was. If he noticed her absence too long after nightfall, he would more than certainly trail after her. And thus far, he has always found her.

Kore made a reluctant retreat to Demeter's side, taking the risk to steal a glance at the path she was to take. Nothing but empty darkness filled her vision. It was an eerie reminder of a dream that was not as long ago as it felt.

She sucked in a breath and sat atop one of her trunks, digging her elbows into the tops of her knees to rest her chin in her hands. As if finding a sound mind and heart weren't hard enough alone. Now she had to wait it all out with an audience.

She released a mindless sigh as she sunk into her space.

"Is unloading trunks a bore to you, Kore?" Ares scoffed. He tugged one of his overly-sized trunks from the cart with a grunt. To even his surprise, it came out with ease but toppled off the back of the chariot sending a loud thud to echo through the still silence as the trove of weapons crashed to the ground.

Kore glared at him through narrowed eyes. Biting her tongue from the response she wished to share. Instead, she reached her arm out and gripped the first leather handle she could. Without breaking eye contact with the god, she yanked the near-weightless trunk from the cart at her side.

It landed in dirt with a loud thud that echoed through the

vast space around them. With nothing standing to absorb their sounds, it was left with an emptiness that told them, at least it told her and Demeter, that life was slim to none. She could only hope it was just bare of civilians and frozen over from the winter as Sparta was.

By the time they had their new camp set up, Ares had drunk down three whole *amphori* of wine. It was a wonder how he got his shelter set up at all, then again, it looked a lot less put together than it usually did – which it was never that clean around his cot or makeshift tent anyway. But he generally had things leveled out and even on both ends. Something he would have to deal with in the morning.

Unfortunately for Kore, his intoxicated self was something she had to endure through dinner. Again.

With the flames dancing in the pit, Demeter prepared all her cooking tools and supplies to get started on yet another stew. Kore felt she would much rather choke down the thick, overpowering sweetness of ambrosia than have to slurp down another serving of the liquid dish. Not that there was anything wrong with them, but every day? Kore's tongue was begging for variety.

"Is there anything else we can make, Mama?" Kore whined. They had checked the rivers and ponds enough during their last visit to assume the waters had cleared and life had returned again. That was, if death hadn't returned to it as well. Fish was an option and wasn't a meat Demeter often opposed to.

"Such as what, my Daisy?" Demeter giggled back as she placed the variety of vegetables onto the flat stone beside the fire.

"I am not sure, possibly fish from the pond. Bread even. I am awfully full of stew," she admitted kindly. Despite the caution in her tone, Demeter's brows fell slightly with a small pinch between them.

"Perhaps, another night after you have fetched the fish. This night, after a long day of travel, I would like to make something simple." Demeter continued arranging the ingredients in preparation for chopping. Her response wasn't surprising and Kore figured it to be the answer. Besides, she hadn't meant for the meal to change that moment, she simply wanted more options. She gave her mother a soft nod and returned to watching the flames. It was a perfect distraction to the wine-guzzling god across the pit, pouring back his fourth *amphora* of the night.

Where he was getting it was beyond Kore, she assumed he had a few trunks full of them since they seemingly never dwindled.

"I still have plenty of that s-stag left. It's dried but if we toss it into the stew —"

"Absolutely not!" Demeter snapped. Ares tossed his hands up in defense with a teasing smile, just as Hermes would.

Grabbing the *amphora*, Ares stood and wobbled his way over to Kore's side. The heavy scent of wine seeped from him as he plopped down in the dirt, missing the log altogether. Demeter's gaze snapped up to him, locking with a great intensity that burned even Kore's side, but she said nothing.

Chop. The sound of the blade hitting the flat stone seemed to echo louder through the space, almost as if it were a threat. But Ares was in his own world trying to situate himself in the new spot. After a moment of deciding which side of him to set the *amphora*, he turned to Kore with hooded, glossy eyes.

"You know, meat is-s not all that bad. Perhaps-s if you had just a tas-ste you would s-see. In fact, I will teach you to hunt."

Chop. The blade smacked the stone again.

"No thank you. I am alright with the diet I have," Kore informed, though a part of her was still curious as to the taste of meat, it did smell delicious and often looked much more appetizing than the stews. After it was cooked of course. Kore did well to avoid watching the cleaning but when the delicious scents twisted about the camp, sometimes she couldn't help but take a peek.

"Come now, Kore," Ares pushed, sliding the top of his hand down Kore's arm.

Chop.

A heavy rock formed in her stomach and the contact was always uncomfortable and unwelcome. But this time, it left a tingling trail behind, one that she hated to acknowledge as enjoyable. Still, she scooted down the log until she was well out of reach of him but he followed.

"Your skin is covered in bumps, you must be so cold," he slurred.

Chop.

"It is cold during the winter." She shrugged boredly, keeping her gaze on the fire.

"That it is. I cannot imagine a fire is too wise inside that fort there. You must suffer greatly at night from the cold."

"I manage just fine."

He chuckled softly, sliding another finger down her arm. The knife slammed down on the stone as Demeter glared at him. Her fingers clawed into the sides of the flat board as hatred seethed from her. Ares chuckled again and dropped his hand.

"Perhaps you would be warmer in my cot," he whispered in attempt to shield his words from Demeter, but they were heard.

The goddess shot up like a towering shadow cast across the grass during the setting sun. Her hands gripped the fabric of her robes as heated words balled on her tongue, ready to unleash whatever evils she had been holding back on him. But all he did was smile back at her with another chuckle.

"Kore!" Demeter began, but Kore was already on her feet, stepping over to her mother's side.

Ares flicked his hands out as if to wave the goddesses off before folding them tightly over his chest. "Fine. I suppose I'll sleep alone then." He released an irritated and exaggerated sigh before muttering, "All this and I cannot even get a simple delight from it."

"What was that?" Demeter roared.

Ares turned to her casually, as if he hadn't spoken. "Kore, has your mother ever told you of Metis? A powerful goddess, much like you –"

"Perhaps, I shall eat in the comfort of my cot."

"That is enough, Ares!"

The women snapped simultaneously. Ares chuckled again before looking down to his lap, "A story for another time then."

Kore would prefer not to hear any stories from the God of War, most certainly not on any goddess that his father tormented out of some invisible fear he had. On top of it all, she didn't want him comparing her power – a power he hadn't seen fully – to that of another, or even insinuating in front of Demeter that her powers were more than they seemed.

"Perhaps you should take your tales to your tent, and stay there for the night," Demeter suggested, to which Ares gave another half-hearted shrug. He made no motion aside from taking another gulp from the *amphora*, not bothering to leave the warmth of the fire to return to his tent.

The remainder of the night was spent hovering near Demeter and the flames, well out of reach from the drunk god who eventually passed out on the log. When they were sure he was deep in his slumber, they retreated to their warm tree fort.

Unlike Ares's assumptions, there was a decent fire, fed and warming the space for their return. With heated cots and furs calling her name, Kore fell face-first into the soft pile of comfort.

CHAPTER XI

OUR EMOTIONS AFFECT OUR WORK

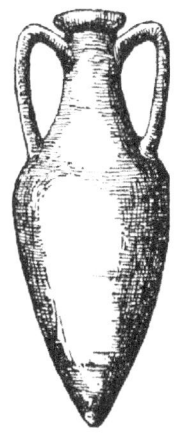

Due to Winter's end the tasks of collecting soil for compost, filling an *amphora* full of water from the nearest river or spring, and plotting their mending plans, were somewhat frivolous. They had already plotted where things would grow on their last visit, and the soil was too hardened by winter to gather. The only thing left was collecting water, and that was if she could locate a body of it that was not already frozen over.

Luckily, their work truly had not been destroyed all that much. Now that the sun was up, and the vast city open for them, she could see the few patches that were horribly damaged and a select few that just didn't seem to take to their gifts as well. Giving her a sense of relief when it came to the spot where the crocus had wilted.

The welcoming scent of freshly baked bread tugged at her as she readied for her day. When she stepped out the stone slab her mother had been using as a table was covered in many different kinds of buns.

Even with her attention over the dough she was kneading, Demeter managed to question Kore. "Will you be off to do your tasks, my Daisy?" Her face, neck, and shoulders were coated in dusty fingerprints, and smears of dried dough clung to her wrists and hands. The usual mess Kore found Demeter in when she made an overabundance of bread.

"With the first winter nearing its end, the soil that houses the newly damaged crops is not fit for compost. I thought I'd look over the fields we tended when we were last here," Kore informed.

Demeter continued with the dough without looking up as she spoke, "I am sure not all of the land you have tended are barren."

Kore stood frozen for a moment until Demeter finally glanced up at her. She smoothed out her features and pinned a forced smile to her face so her mother wouldn't see the concern filling her.

"It would not hurt for me to check while I am walking about." Kore shrugged and crossed to the table for a bun. "I will collect the soil while I am out."

Demeter sighed and returned her gaze to the dough. "Since you will be going far, please be safe. I am sure you do not want Ares with you." Demeter turned up again and Kore nodded frantically.

The Goddess of Harvest giggled, "In that case, you should get going before he starts stomping around the camp."

The forced smile dropped instantly. Kore snatched up another bun and spun around to march off before Ares could stir. She slung the sack over her shoulder as she began her small journey along the empty path to the closest patch Demeter had worked.

As she walked, she considered placing another crocus – or attempting to do as such. Since the death was not spreading off to the other plants, she felt well enough to try again. After all, her lavender sprouts were getting better by the day.

Demeter had always told her that their emotions weighed greatly on their work. At the meadow, Kore purposefully sought out means to release her anger during a time of frustration. She hadn't yet experienced the suffocating emotions that weighed on her in the field. She hadn't yet had an experience so hollowing that it negatively affected her work when she was trying to do good. She hadn't been forced to experience it all without means of release—now she was.

A small weight lifted from her shoulders, drifting away with the faint breeze of fresh grass and drifting cypress. She was in the mortal realm to work and bring about life once more, and that is what she planned to do. She could not afford to wilt anything else. Not only to avoid suspicion but to do what she promised.

She knew the sooner they mended the land, the sooner she could return to the meadow and unleash her frustrations on her own planted clones. All she had to do was push back the plaguing visions of her vengeful vines working out of her control.

The pressure began to weigh on her chest once again as the thought alone sent her heart racing.

I have control. I have control of my emotions and my powers. She reminded herself. It helped somewhat, but the lingering guilt still weighed heavily on her heart.

She broke off bits of bread, chewing it slowly to register every slight flavor and texture. Anything to busy her mind from the internal noise that raged in her head.

The sound of songbirds grew as she neared the patch of cypress trees her mother had cared for. Their branches held steady and their needle-like leaves brightened upon her presence.

"Pleasant morning to you," she greeted with a beaming smile. One she did not have to force. Trees held more wisdom over the others. Possibly because they had lived longer lives than the grass, flowers, and bushes around them. Taking in the world through a different lens, they had always seemed more forgiving and understanding in Kore's extra gifts.

They understood the movements of mortals and anticipated the motivations of the divines. They were patient and soft with her no matter her discretion or vengeance.

"How are we doing on this fine day?" She cooed again, coming to a stop before the first tree, digging her heels into the surprisingly soft soil. Warmed and nourished by the living magic of the tree's roots.

"I am here to check the fine soil." She looked back up to the tree with a hopeful smile, "As long as it is alright with you, of course."

The cypress flared its needles with a slight shift in color as they graciously approved of her task.

"Thank you, my dear friends. I have to hurry though, so I am afraid I cannot linger and enjoy your shade. I must check the other grounds worked during our last visit," she informed as she scooped up handfuls of the soil to dump in the sack.

The cypress and bushes at its trunk wiggled and waved in response, ensuring her that all was mended with the land. Aside from a lone patch they could not seem to reach. Though they did not appear all that worried about it, Kore questioned them on the location to give it a quick inspection. "Which direction would this be in?"

The cypress needles and blades of grass shifted west with a sudden turn of wind. They waved their branches in a movement so slight, most would not have caught it. She followed the indicated direction west to her questionable flower grave.

Her chest tightened as she gazed at the familiar line of trees. Of course, they would be referring to the patch where she burnt the crocus.

She sighed again, not surprised or even disappointed. She knew it was something she would have to fix, but she felt less stressed about it knowing the trees that worked with her mother didn't suspect or know that Kore had been the one to cause it. As long as she can work with it without her mother's knowledge, she could do so stress-free. With all else, Demeter's disapproval was the last thing she needed chewing at her mind.

"Perhaps I will take a look." Kore heaved the sack of soil over her shoulder. "First, I must take this here soil to Mama. I thank you for it and the directions." She waved her goodbyes before hurrying back to their shelter. The thin stream of smoke reached high into the sky, signaling the beginning of the evening when Demeter took to preparing their supper.

Kore tilted her head up to the blazing sun, measuring the distance it still had before dipping behind the far-off trees and hills. Not long enough for a steady walk back if she wanted to reach the patch before the day's light came to a swift end.

She marched off, beginning the short but grueling journey back. One thing she did not like about being out of her meadow, was the walking paths along the fields. Stretches of dry, abrasive sands cluttered with jagged rocks that bit into her feet with almost every step.

With the war and decay, she was aware the lands would be dry, but didn't consider the vengeful nature of it. The soil and paths back in the meadow were rich and soft, making for a soothing journey with each step.

Back home, cuts and slices were not an issue that marred her feet. Now it was such a consistent occurrence, she was considering asking Demeter about thicker sandals. Despite her mother's suggestions to pack a few more pairs before they had left the comfort of their meadow.

When Kore thought about it, the mortal world outside her mother's trees was harsh and full of things with jagged, painful edges. From the rocks to the dirt, the grass, and trees. All of them had a roughness to them that the meadow never experienced.

The smell of burning wood grew stronger as she neared the fire. Thankfully, Demeter ensured the land around their fort was well-nourished and enriched with life. This made it much more soothing to Kore's feet as she stepped through it to place the sack down by their compost pile.

Demeter had used the morning to set the boundaries of

the pile with sticks. Weaving long, thick strips of bark around the branches to keep the soil from spilling free.

Kore shook out the soreness of her arms, scanning the empty area for her mother or even Ares. Not that she minded them both absent, it meant she didn't have to inform or explain where she was headed.

Less bread lined the table than what was placed that morning but Kore noticed the lone fig and cheese *plakous* drizzled with sweet golden honey. She gave another glance around before snatching up the sweet treat and skipping out of the gentle soil. A motion that came to an instant halt when her feet touched the rougher grass. She groaned around the bite full of *plakous* she was enjoying to tread carefully over the brittle blades.

Pools of golden sun stretched before her. Cast out from gaps in the branches and leaves. Shades of purple and pink painted the sky above in a beautiful wash of color. The familiar scent of cypress mixed with a fleeting scent that had caught in the breeze.

Kore tilted her head back, drawing in a deep breath to catch the smell once more. She brought the plakous to her lips, taking in another whiff.

Fig and honey. The fleeting smell had been from her sweet pastry. She took a bite, savoring the flavor and feeling it brought for when she would have to wait to taste it again.

She could not discern the mix of emotions that washed over her. A bitter sorrow mixed with a familiar pining of something unreachable. She continued along the path the grass had made for her while trying to put a name to what it was.

The *plakous* touched her lips again as she went for another bite, chewing slowly as she thought.

It was on the tip of her tongue and just as she felt the word brewing, she found herself in the silent, lifeless patch. The emptiness it brought forced her to push back the desiderium that was beginning to overcome her.

"I have returned," she whispered, looking over the earth. The same hollow feeling burrowed through her. The cypress wavered, the curve in its trunk relaxed. Branches swayed in a faint rhythm. The vibrations of it tickled her feet as it traveled from her toes to her legs and chest then arms. Their words filled her in a comforting tune. It continued its travel up her neck and through her cheeks until it paused between her ears, where the vibrations turned to words.

You cannot ignore what is within you.

It was the first time she had heard them in such audible clarity, it caused her to jump at the sound. A discovery she desperately wanted to explore more of, but she was there to figure out what to do with the patch, she would have plenty of time to learn about her new way of communication soon. Regardless, what she did know was that their sudden words were right.

She cupped her hands together, as she often did, to pull the clone. The once brief moments she took to center herself and draw concentration were now lengthened for her to find a sense of peace without guilt. Replacing the thought of her failures and vines with the warm comforting feeling the plakous brought. The joy she felt in hearing the words from the trees. It was the unforced joy she needed. A reminder of the happiness her powers brought.

A golden glow emitted from her palms as the creation formed, the low humming and cooling sensation filled her hands as the lavender came to be. Finally, she had managed to bring forth something, and it was her most perfect creation. The purple petals were vibrant. The stem, thick and strong. Even the dangly roots were a bright and lively shade.

Her shoulders relaxed as she gazed at the beautiful flower, ready for planting. But first, she needed to replenish the dirt with live soil. She placed the sprout along the roots of the tree to search the soil around her, collecting from the nearby trees and plants as they offered their bounty to her.

She skipped from trunk to trunk, overjoyed that her powers were not depleted. Her mother had mentioned a few times when her powers had failed her and faltered a task. But she never lingered on such talks, and it was clear to Kore the faults were not ones Demeter cared to recount. Perhaps it was fate for the divines to struggle at times. She was young after all, and in the middle of a great transition as both a goddess and woman. Her powers were likely to obscure at times, she just wished it wasn't during an imperative moment in her proving herself as a divine and not just the youngest, last-born child of Zeus.

With the soil collected, Kore worked on mixing it into the starving dirt, churning it down with her fingers to soften it for the coming roots. When everything was to a moist, rich mixture, Kore placed the plant, roots first, into the dimpled hole. She gave the soil around its stem a gentle pat to ensure stability and watched as the lavender wiggled happily in place, stretching its roots out along the softened earth.

"Much better. Let me collect a bit of water for you, I will be right back." Kore hopped up and sprinted back to the shelter to collect the *amphora* of water. Her mother had returned to the fire and was busy with her back to Kore. Normally she would have addressed her, but she was in a rush to return to the lavender. She snatched the *amphora*, happy it was half full for the lug back. She wasn't able to sprint but she mustered up a decent speed as she marched back to the trees.

"Alright," she huffed as she worked at the cork of the clay, "I have returned with your water." She paused before the tree, the aching silence burned her ears, giving way for the hollowing feeling to return. It hit her gut first before she even thought to look down, the creeping feeling of death filled the air.

Her eyes shot to the cause. The bright and sturdy lavender lay limp in the dirt, its leaves fading to a powdery purple and its stem just as dull. Kore dropped the *amphora*, filling the silent air with a harsh echoing shatter. A soft whimper escaped her as the tears welled up in her eyes and the sinking weight pressed hard against her lungs.

Even if it was a fault in her powers due to her age, it wasn't something she could hide much longer. The drowning fear that it was something that would stay with her was becoming too much to hold onto without guidance. The thought of it felt as if someone drove a blade through her chest. She had been trying to avoid it. Playing nice with Ares to keep him quiet about it. But now, she had only one option left.

I need my mama.

It was a defeat she didn't want to face, but she no longer had the choice. With one last sigh, she turned from the dying patch to head back to her mother. Explanations and outcomes played through her mind the entire way. She thought on what she would say, what she could say, what lies would work or how she could display it without fully admitting to her hand in it. None of which seemed to go in a way she'd want and all ended in her mother's disappointment.

The smoke from the fire pit had widened, a sign Kore had come to learn meant the iron pot had been placed and supper was in the making. She had, at most, a few moments to inform her mother before Ares stomped in with his kill of the day.

When she had left the patch, the sun was nestled snugly in the treetops, but when she made it to the blazing fire pit, the sky was a dark shade of deep blue with a mix of gray clouds that seemed to be smeared over the waking stars.

The loud crackle and pop of the burning log mixed with the repeating scraping of the wooden spoon to the iron. Demeter stood above a steaming pot with angry flames reaching over the mouth. The heated moisture had clung to the goddess's hair, shaping Demeter's usually uniform curls into a tangled mess.

It was a look of stress and overstimulation from the day that Kore was well familiar with and she knew the news of the patch would only bring Demeter more things to worry on. But Kore could not bring herself to lie about this on top of so many other things.

Not anymore.

"Mama," she whispered somberly. Demeter continued stirring the mix of ingredients in the pot. Her lips curved into a smile that did not reach her eyes. The grating sound of wood on iron continued to scream out against the sudden extreme silence of the night.

She sighed, but did not look up as she spoke, "Yes, my

Daisy?"

    Kore inhaled deeply to fight the sudden nervousness that twisted her stomach. "There is a patch, out by the trees I have been mending," Kore began.

    The nagging noise of wood to iron was disrupted for a brief moment, but Demeter continued to stir. "And what of this plot?"

    Kore's gaze danced between her mother and the wooden spoon in the stew as the scraping continued to echo louder and louder into the night. It seemed as though it was drowning out Kore's own thoughts.

    "Well, it does not seem to want to accept our mending and has rejected any clone sprout I placed in it." Her words rushed from her lips, the sour burn of the half-lie coated her tongue.

    Demeter's eyes slowly climbed up to meet Kore's. "How do you mean?"

    "I have tried mending it myself, but it does not seem to want to accept my energy. I was hoping maybe you could take a look and offer it yours." Kore shrugged innocently.

    Heat burst from the fire as it flared up, gripping the iron handles as if to react with her mother's emotions. Demeter moved around the pit without care or fear of its touch. Her eyes locked on Kore as she came to stand just an inch away.

    Heat engulfed her cheek with the lingering scent of cypress as a warm hand covered her. Demeter's comforting touch calmed the young goddess, but only for a moment.

    "Where is this?" Demeter asked.

    Warm, dry air filled Kore's lungs. Scratching her throat from the smoke that circled them. Fighting the wave of coughs that begged to release, Kore pointed behind her in the direction of the field and offered a brief description of where Demeter would find it.

    "Alright. I will take a look tomorrow morning. It will be a nice lesson for you. We haven't had one in some time, it will be a decent practice," Demeter beamed pridefully. A feeling Kore wished to have, instead, her compunction over it began to weigh on her.

CHAPTER XII

THE PHANTOM FLOWERS

"Your practice has done wonders, my Dear," Demeter praised as she watched Kore craft a replicated oak sapling. After patting the soil down, Kore looked up to her mother with a cheery smile. Thankfully, after a few moons of consistent strenuous practice with her mother's guidance, her craft had returned. Allowing her to clone the vegetation once again. It had been twice as long since her vines had approached her and though she missed their closeness, their absence had lifted a dreadful weight from her shoulders for the time.

Without the worry of them breaking free or doing as they pleased, she was able to focus on the life she could bring, and with the ending of their second Winter upon them, she had even less time to prepare for the Spring. Demeter was most determined to have Kore work the season on her own this go and being that Kore wanted to help, she agreed.

Over the past Summer, Kore and Demeter had worked over the patch to return life to the soil with no luck. Demeter had yet to figure out the reason and had turned to ignoring it for the time, but only because she was pushing Kore as hard as she was for Spring. She had the utmost confidence that Kore would be able to mend it once she was able to pull a sprout herself without cloning it. Holding no clue that Kore was the cause of the entire thing. A secret the young goddess planned to keep to herself until absolutely necessary and since the decay didn't seem to be spreading, she found no reason to share just yet.

Kore visited the patch often, working her clones into the dry earth only to watch them instantly wilt and fall limp. Ares tagged along a few times, finding the entire study a bore since he wasn't able to witness her vines. After a while, he began avoiding it whenever Kore mentioned that working on it was her day's plan. Not that she could truly enjoy the distance.

Once back at the comfort of the warm fires, he found a near-nightly routine to hover over her. Most of the time she was lucky if he didn't drown himself in wine, but when he did, he had grown uncomfortably and overly touchy. Mostly knee taps and arm bumps, nothing too noticeable from Demeter's point, but Kore knew it to be deliberate.

"Winter is drawing near. You will have plenty of time to prepare for Spring. Hopefully, the abundance will aid that curious patch. I fear whatever horrors befell it is a powerful one. Some mortals love to meddle in things they should not. Always poisoning our gifts with their war and bloodshed," Demeter droned.

It was something Kore knew was coming for her, being the Goddess of Spring, she needed to start taking control of it on her own. It was just an inconvenient time for Demeter to want her to take it on alone.

Though she was elated about her progress in cloning, Kore's heart sank at Demeter's words, but she continued to hold the forced smile on her lips despite the pain it began to cause her cheeks. Every day was a reminder of the moment getting closer.

If not from her mother, then it was from the plants and trees. "Perhaps that is not as wonderful as it would seem," Kore muttered under her breath.

Demeter popped her head up over the fire, "What was that, Dear?"

"Nothing," Kore rushed.

A smile pulled at the corner of Demeter's lips, blissfully unaware of her daughter's secrets. Which was for the best in Kore's case, the last thing she needed was her mother fussing over her as she did back at the meadow. Independence had slowly been granted to her over the last few moons and she didn't want to undo all that by worrying her mother.

It wasn't as if Demeter could help anyway. Without the truth of the cause, Demeter would never truly know what to do to fix the patch. She did not know of Kore's vines, or their tendency to have a mind of their own. She did not know of Kore's true powers. How could she ever help what she could not see and what she could not know?

Kore was alone.

Well, not entirely. The only one she felt could understand her was also the only one who knew of her true power. But *he* was unreachable and even if he were, what could he do to help? His very presence would send her mother into a questioning fit.

The stew sloshed into her *kylix*, sending a few drops of the scolding liquid onto her wrist, pulling her from her troubling thoughts over the past moons back to her mother's fret-filled eyes.

"Are you well, Dear?"

Kore blinked at Demeter for a moment before snapping another forced smile on her lips.

"All is well, Mama," she assured brightly, "I am just thinking about Spring, is all." She shook off the liquid as she spoke, pretending as if the heat hadn't bothered her. The night was stressful enough without her mother pawing over her and a slight burn.

"Ah yes. Lovely Spring. Just a moon away. Have you

decided on what you will focus on first?" Demeter gushed proudly. Her insouciant enthusiasm was palpable and commendable but wasted because Kore had no clue what she planned to do with the upcoming Spring. And she could only wish to feel about it the same as her mother did.

As they headed back to camp, Kore thought of all the ways she could try and invest herself into the title as she took a seat on a petrified fallen log. Ways she could learn and grow in her powers. But no matter how bright she wanted that plan to be, it was foreshadowed by the threat of her unpredictable vines.

While she thought, she ate. Almost mechanically as she ignored the scolding burn that filled her mouth and seared her throat. She was aware of the pain but not present with it as she took another spoonful of steaming stew into her mouth.

Perhaps if I found a way to be as I was in the meadow. I may have been trapped in the confines of the trees, but I was free to roam. I had my privacy and I had… my vines. I just need to find that spark again.

A spark would be easier to find if she had some semblance of normalcy – or what she had considered normalcy to be for her. She made up a mental list of all the activities and things that brought her joy at the meadow. Aside from Lotus, there were the goats, the chickens, the winding maze of a forest, and the spring she had spent so much of her time at.

There was no Lotus to turn to and no goats or chickens to talk about her troubles with. There were no thick forests with twisting trunks. And there were scarcely any springs for her to swim in. Even if there were, she wasn't looking to freeze in them.

There was, however, one thing she had not done in years, mostly because she was no longer a little girl, light on the branches. Oh, but how the sudden longing rained down on her. It was a peace and comfort she found in the trees. Their mutual understanding and long-lasting knowledge. She craved their wisdom, now more than ever.

She was no longer a little girl. Her worries and troubles surpassed that of being told to practice her raspberries. It had been too long since she last confided in them in such a way.

Another blazing sip raced down her throat as she finished off the stew. Her mother's wide eyes looked over Kore as she took her place at her side.

"I thought you would at least enjoy your meal," she muttered with a teasing hint to her tone. Kore giggled as she looked between Demeter's full bowl and her empty one.

"Oh!" she gasped mindlessly, "Well, I did enjoy it."

Had she taken time to be present in her meal, she would have enjoyed it. She always had. But this time, her mind was up in the treetops.

"I was just thinking about what I wanted to start my work on for the Spring."

Demeter perked up, a smile spreading her lips, "That is wonderful, my Daisy. What may that be?"

"I wanted to start with the trees. I was thinking I would spend some time with them to see what they enjoy and gather their perspective," Kore explained. It was more truth than a lie. She did plan to spend time with them and gather their thoughts on the upcoming season. But she also wanted their view on her hesitations with it.

Demeter looked around them with searching eyes before she lowered her voice to a whisper, "If you want. But you must find a day when Ares leaves for hunting or leave before Helios rises for his duty if you want to go it alone and without…" Her eyes shot up passed Kore and her expression twisted. She straightened herself in her seat as she spoke in a dry, monotone voice. "Ares."

"Demeter. Kore. Sorry I'm late for supper. No stew for me though." He pulled a rope with several wild rabbits attached to it. "I caught my own!"

Up to five poor, furry creatures, strung up by their feet with their wide lifeless eyes staring right into Kore's soul. The stew churned in her stomach as bile bubbled up in her throat.

Kore covered her mouth and nose as she jumped to her feet. "Excuse me. I am going to be sick," she said dryly before heading to the tree fort.

Ares frequently skinned his captures by the fire, he wasn't clean or gentle about it. Ripping and slicing with a single blade.

Unfortunately for Kore, she had witnessed him in this process a few times. The sight alone caused her stomach to tighten, and there were sounds and smells she couldn't rid her mind of. One always brought with it the other. She kept her hand over her nose and pushed at the wooden door with her shoulder.

Once it closed behind her, she sucked in a deep breath of fresh cypress air. The heated shelter caressed her chilled cheeks, warming them instantly. She flexed her fingers and toes, feeling the effects of the unforgivable weather. It would certainly make her work for the following day much harder to do if all she could focus on was the icy bites at her skin the entire time.

To prepare for the early rise, she set out the longer, thicker robes her mother so graciously thought to bring, along with her leather sandals. She set the robes neatly over the back bar of her cot and set the sandals on the floor beside it.

After adding a peplos for good measure, Kore took a seat at the small table in the back to admire her mother's sproutlings.

It wasn't long before the pleasant smell of Ares's cooked kill began drifting into the fort, twisting around her nose. Her stomach tightened, hungry for more than just a liquid diet.

Fish was no longer an option, being so far and with no supply to be found. The lakes and ponds were frozen over. Vegetables and what they could forage was all they had access to so far out, leaving them with the simple stew once more.

A low creak filled the space as Demeter pushed open the heavy door. Her full *kylix* of stew in hand.

Clearly, Kore was not the only one who couldn't stomach the skinning or cooking that was being conducted.

"If you were thinking of having more stew, do not," Demeter warned flatly. Kore's face fell instantly. She was tired of it but she was planning on having a bit more before she ended her night. Now she could only assume it was ruined.

"He put the meat in it?"

"I offered another cooking pot, but –"

"Why dirty up another pot when there is one right here?" Kore deepened her voice to mimic what she knew Ares to have said. It was the same reasoning every time he sullied their meals.

With a heavy sigh, she pushed her bowl to the center of the table and made her way to her cot for the night. She didn't much care to go outside and wash up the *kylix*, to be set with Ares alone when he started on his wine. Even the smallest amount of time he'd find a way to crowd her with questions and rough hands.

CHAPTER XIII

A LOST BOY AND THE GODDESS OF LOVE

The frigid air continued to nip at Kore's cheeks, only growing colder the higher she climbed. She didn't quite make it to the top of the old tree. Most of its thickest and most stable branches were in the middle of the towering pine. One, in particular, was angled perfectly for her to view the fields all around without obstacles.

After a few dragging days with Ares over her shoulder, she had finally convinced him to take a night and enjoy himself with wine. Demeter never allowed Kore the drink and advised against her ploy but Kore pretended to drink along with him, switching her *amphora* out with water. Drunk as planned, Ares slept well into the morning, allowing Kore to escape to the bare branch trees.

    She rested her head back, drinking in the tender memories that flooded her mind. So many special moments in her life happened at the top of the trees in her mother's meadow, some changing her life to shape her into who she was.

    Memories of the dark-robed king and his expression of confusion as he was lost in her mother's field. The fallen boy she hadn't thought about in such a long time. She had never learned of what his name was, where he was coming from, or what he was doing. Why he fashioned himself wings made of wood, feathers, and wax. She wondered where his placement in the Underworld ended up being but most of all she wondered why he decided to fly in the first place.

    Hermes had always told her flying was freeing in a way most would never understand. Being able to sore high and low, far and wide with no shackles holding him to the ground.

    It was something Kore could never do, metaphorically or physically. She wished to experience the feeling of freedom and liberation, but she was stuck on earth, shackled by both her powers. A constant battle inside her, such is life and death.

    A battle.

    For so long she understood the balance, but that was when she had a decent one. Now – now she was all over the place.

    Her eyes fluttered open to take in the clear blue sky above. No soring, screaming boys dotted the horizon this day. Only the dark smoke of the dwindling war smeared the heavens. It was too far to tell from her distance but that only meant if it were a battle, they were far enough away to not give too much worry.

    She relaxed her head back against the bark of the tree, closing her eyes once more. Her hands gripped the peplos that was wrapped tightly around her and she snuggled into the warmth it provided.

    It wasn't early anymore, the sun was nearing its highest point and her mother had been out tending a field with a few bushes that needed her attention. Thankfully, Ares had not stirred yet, his snore was loud enough to carry to Kore's perch in the trees. It was annoying but easily ignored while her mind spun with what to speak of first.

The trees were patient as she collected her thoughts, pushing encouraging vibrations into her palm as she patted the lively bark. Though, the time for them to communicate to her with words was short-lived, she didn't let it detour her from seeking their guidance. "I never thought I'd lose control of them," she began, "My vines that is. They have always had their own consciousness but have always done as I bid. But this time, it was as if my word meant nothing, my power, my control. They did not heed it. And now, if I am not careful with my emotions, I could ruin all Mama and I have worked for."

The branches stirred, sending their questions in calming vibrations to ask when else had her powers betrayed her.

"Back in Sparta. Everything I attempted came out... wrong and I –" Suddenly the silent air was cut by a shrieking cry that echoed from her right. She snapped her attention to the small meadow, hidden behind the wall of trees, to the spring she had ventured on their first visit. Frozen over now that winter had touched it.

Her eyes scanned the spaces between the trunks, trying to locate the source of the cry as it rang through the air again. She turned back to the camp to see if the screams carried as far as Demeter, but her mother continued to work unbothered just as Ares's snores continued without fail.

The screams rang again, this time she could tell it was most distinctively a crying child. She spun around, already lifting to make her way down the tree when she spotted him.

A small boy clung to the broken ice of the pond, his lower body submerged.

"Mama!" Kore called out, jumping the rest of the way down. She didn't have time to see if her mother had heard or even run to get her, she needed to act fast to save the boy before it was too late.

Her peplos snagged on a low-hanging branch as she sprinted through the trees, ripping and tearing as it was yanked off her. She left it as she ducked and weaved through the outreaching branches. Frigid air burned her lungs as she heaved each breath, but she continued to push her legs, cold and numb already from the chill. The boy's screams and cries continued to pull her toward the pond. Louder and louder they grew as she cleared the last of the trees.

Her heart plummeted to her stomach as her eyes landed on the boy, slipping in the last moment of her arrival. He cried out again in a shaking small voice, "It's cold." As the words left his purpling lips, his hands gave out. He clawed at the ice but the water seemed to have sucked him under.

She was late but still had time to fish him out. With another painful huff, she ran over to the edge of the pond where the brittle ice began cracking and breaking apart from the splashing of the boy. He had fallen in too far from the edge and walking across would risk Kore falling in as well.

She had one option.

She snapped her eyes shut and lifted her hands. "Please help," she begged. But she only felt stillness under her feet.

"Please!" she begged again in earnest. Tears began spilling over her cheeks as air ripped from her lungs. The vines churned the icy soil under her feet but did not surface.

The boy continued to splash, and claw at the ice, each resurface sucked him down and he was taking in too much water.

"I'm sorry! I'm sorry!" She shouted to both the boy and her vines, but still the vines remained under her. She strained against them, pulling at them as if she was pulling an unmovable boulder. Her teeth ground down so hard she feared she may break them, but she didn't stop or ease up on her call.

"Please, my vines. He needs us – he needs you... *I* need you!" She pleaded with them, begging for their support before too late but still, they were silent.

The ice was thin, cracking along the trail the boy took to get to the center, leaving half of the surface too unstable to tread. Kore ran to the more solid half, still pulling at her vines for help, but now it was on her. She had to rely on herself.

Words from an old story Hermes had told her flooded

her mind.

"I had to distribute my weight to retrieve them. Can you believe that, Kore? I couldn't fly to them of course, they were what gave me the ability to fly. Pity Apollo threw them so far out." He had said.

Distribute weight. I need to distribute my weight! She thought as she stepped onto the ice. The cracking and popping echoed loudly through the air, rising above the splashing frantic child.

As quickly and safely as she could, Kore lowered herself onto her stomach and began scooting over the chilling ice.

"I am here. I am coming!" she cried out to the boy. Below her, the popping and cracking intensified. The ice was too thin for even her attempts. It broke away from under her and she was next to be sucked under. The water felt shocking, like a thousand daggers piercing her skin. It froze her chest, making even the smallest attempts to scream a hassle. The churning and splashing from the boy and the weighted fabric of her robes began pulling her deeper.

She desperately tried to grab the ice for support but it was drifting out of her reach. She opened her mouth to project a muffled scream but the chilling water cut her throat with vengeance as it filled her mouth.

The boy continued to struggle above her, the distance growing between them. Her lungs squeezed and cried for air that would not come. The small beam of light that came through the hole began to grow smaller and darker. She tried to kick, but her legs felt as if they were moving through mud rather than water. She grew weak with every second. Unable to fight, and soon unable to move.

With the little bit of strength she had, she called to her vines one last time before the world around her fell dark and silent. The cold was gone and she felt… nothing. A muffled sound broke through the thick slosh of ice. At first, it was disoriented and indistinguishable. Slowly, it cleared as it pushed through the barrier.

You must remember the balance. A dual voice echoed. It

wasn't clear, but it wasn't gargled from bubbles. Kore looked around the dark space, finding nothing of distinguishable interest to cause the sound.

Remember the balance. The voices sounded again, this time, they were much clearer and closer. And where there was once nothing but darkness around her, she was soon surrounded by warmth, though the lighting was only slightly brighter, she felt comforted. She felt safe and she didn't feel alone.

A far-off shadow figure drifted her way. The water around her continued to shift in the slow tide it made and above her was the dim light that blurred out the ice and hole, even the boy had vanished in the engulfing depth of the water. Her attention fell back on the nearing shadow, its head dipped low to shield its ghostly face.

"Hello?" Kore called clearly, the water an invisible obstacle.

This is surely death I have discovered.

The figure stopped inches from Kore with its head still hung low and out of view. "You must remember." The dual voices sounded again as the shadow held out a transparent hand.

"Remember what?" Kore asked. Her chest felt heavier with each passing second but she continued to wait. Finally, the figure lifted its head to present itself to her. When the phantom hair drifted from view, Kore sucked in a sharp gasp, staring at herself through the thin haze of what she now saw as disillusion.

Without any further warning, it reached out and gripped Kore by the hand, "Without death, there is no true life." The voices fell on Kore's ears as a horrifying growl. She yanked back, thrashing through the icy water once more.

Her lungs burned for air, screaming for her to inhale, but she pressed her lips tight. Blinded by the violent slosh of bubbles, Kore called to whatever she could feel around her.

The chilling icy water bit and burned the tips of her fingers and toes. She opened her mouth to release a scream only to be instantly silenced by the flood of water that filled her. Her head grew heavy from the pressure and the water around her began to fade dark once more.

Shattering ice and a thunderous thump mixed the water about until something slipped around Kore's waist. Instant comfort washed over her and the feeling of tranquility filled her chest as the darkness dotted out her vision.

Suddenly, she was jerked up, a tight rope gripping her waist as it flung her out of the water. She landed hard on her side, gasping and spitting up. Her head lolled back, weak, and hair heavy with water that dripped into her eyes. Her vision was blurred with each drop and cleared with each rapid blink while she struggled to focus on the sight before her. The earth groaned with a low rumbling quake as two thick vines whipped in the air before slithering back into the crevice they broke from.

Kore wiped the water from her eyes as she frantically struggled up to catch the tip of the vines just as they vanished completely. Before she could whisper her thanks and praises to them, the boy coughed, choking on the water that filled his lungs and throat. She cocked her head back, finding the child safe on land, far from the broken ice. He convulsed with each hack of the liquid as it drained from his mouth. His blue lips and pale skin shocked her up as she rushed to him.

"Are you well?" she cried, scooping the unknown child into her arms to hold him. Her hands rubbed his back and arms frantically as she tried to warm him up.

"Where are your parents?" she shot again in a shaking voice. The weak boy didn't answer with words, but his teeth chattered loudly.

"Mama!" Kore screamed out again. She didn't release him as he clung to her, crying and shivering from the invasive cold that surrounded them.

"Adonis!" A song-like voice shouted from behind Kore. It was familiar but faintly. She turned to see who had come, and her eyes fell wide as Aphrodite raced to their side. She grabbed the boy in a panic and hugged him to her breast as tears began streaming down her cheeks. She rocked back and forth with him, words of apologies and promises spilled from her mouth. She took her thick, dry peplos from around her shoulders and shrouded the boy with it. Still rubbing his arms just as Kore was.

Finally, after what seemed like hours, Aphrodite turned to her, a look of indignation mixed with a hint of gratitude creased her features.

"*You* saved him?" she said with a shaking voice. Kore nodded. Her teeth clattered together and the shivering came in a full attack.

"Is he yours?" Kore pushed out. Aphrodite looked over Kore from head to toe and without a word, snapped her fingers to drape another thick peplos, smelling of roses and wine, over Kore's shoulders.

"Adonis, you cannot run off like that!" Aphrodite scolded the boy. She brought him back into her, holding him to her chest with great protection.

"In a sense," she gave Kore another curious look. One that seemed as though she was debating on sharing more with her, "His name is Adonis. He is only three winters. I had turned my back for but a moment to grab him something to eat..." Aphrodite trailed off with her explanation.

"Adonis?" Kore repeated. It was awfully close to a name she was familiar with, "Like Aidoneus?"

The words spilled from her mouth mindlessly as she looked over the small child. He was beautiful, with loose ringlet curls as black as night plastered to his forehead and neck.

Aphrodite tilted her head curiously at Kore. "No. He is nothing like that monster," she hissed.

Kore leaned back at the hurtful words. Aidoneus was far from a monster. The reaction puzzled Aphrodite for a moment before the corner of her lips twitched at a smile.

"Oh! You do not find him so monstrous, do you?" The goddess pointed. Kore shook her head sheepishly.

Aphrodite's eyes popped wide, her smile growing, "Awe, you have a softness for the King of the Underworld?"

Kore's heart sank and she shook her head again. Though it was a lie, she didn't need an Olympian holding that information, especially one she knew was close to her mother, even if it was at a point long ago.

"No need to be so coy, Kore. I can sense it. It is like a

scent, you see. Love, that is. It is unmistakable and you are covered in it." She snickered to herself as if she uncovered a useful secret. The last thing Kore wanted was the Goddess of Love holding anything over her, she already didn't seem to care much for Kore. What could she possibly want with the knowledge?

"Ares is still guarding you and your mother. Is that correct?" she asked next. Kore blinked with wide eyes, her mind still on Aidoneus and a secret she thought she'd keep a bit longer. Finally, she nodded to the question.

"Of course he is. Well, if you promise not to tell him about Adonis, I will not mention your fancy for the God of the Dead. To anyone. Do we have a deal?" Aphrodite's beautifully full lips pulled up into a wide smile, but Kore would not call it a friendly one. It was more self-serving as if she was proud of herself for collecting such information. Yet, Kore nodded still.

It wasn't hard to figure out why she would want to keep Adonis from Ares. A secret child with another lover other than himself. The stories her mother shared with her about the two Olympians never ended well when they each found a new obsession to lust over.

A secret for a secret.

Kore opened and closed her mouth, unsure what to say to the goddess. It was a strange place for her to be, unless she was following Ares about, but somehow, that didn't seem to be the cause. If she knew where he was she wouldn't have ensured he was with Kore and Demeter.

A thunderous crack and a following rumbling pop echoed through the fields. Kore spun around to face the direction from which the sound likely came.

Their camp.

When she turned back, Aphrodite had vanished with the boy, leaving her pink, rose-smelling cloud and a slew of questions for Kore to ponder over, behind. Before she could have time to think about the goddess or the boy named Adonis, the next sound that rang through stilled her heart.

"Ares!" Athena roared.

THREE YEARS WITH ARES

CHAPTER XIV

MILK OF THE POPPY

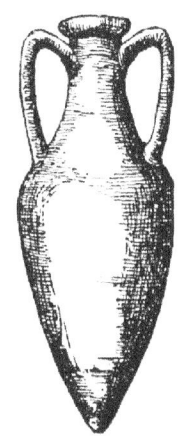

Kore arrived back at the camp to a commotion. Ares held a hand to his head, gold dripping down his temple and cheek. Demeter was busy trying to calm Athena who was seething with rage as she glared at Ares. "What did you do?"

Ares gritted his teeth and bared them at Athena. Gold coated his lips, spitting it out as he spoke, "You came here with accusations and assaults. If you were not my father's favorite, I'd –"

"You would do what? Have him throw me in Tartarus? That is where the four of you belong," Athena snapped, seething anger clouded her otherwise calm demeanor.

"Four?" Demeter gasped, her attention turning to Ares.

"Yes, it would appear Ares, Apollo, Artemis, and Aphrodite all have been conspiring to aid the Trojans. Despite my father's wishes." Athena spun around to Ares with narrowed eyes, "Who's idea was that, Ares? Was it yours? Working anyway you can to spite our father I see."

"*My* father." Ares spat the correction with venom. But Athena maintained an unmoved expression, seemingly board with his statement.

Demeter turned slightly, her eyes locking with Kore. "Oh, my Daisy. How were the trees?" she hurried her words and rushed to Kore's side, her eyes bulging as she took notice of the wet robes and Kore's soaked hair. "My Dear! What happened to you?"

Kore's teeth chattered and her body shook from the chilling breeze. "Th-th-the s-spring," she stuttered out.

Athena and Ares quieted their battle while Demeter hurried Kore to the fire. Once she was settled around it with a dry, thick peplos over her shoulders, their arguing continued.

"*Our* father is not going to be pleased when you return to Olympus. Were you not supposed to be here with Demeter and Kore?" Athena berated. Ares kept the hard crease of irritation on his face as he stared the goddess down.

"Do not presume to speak to me about *my* father and what he will and will not be pleased with. You were nothing more than an *afterthought*. I came from a true binding."

"Pick your next words cautiously, Ares," Athena warned through clenched teeth.

"Now, now. I am sure we can come to a calm understanding," Demeter attempted to sway but they didn't budge or stand down from each other. They were practically nose to nose, heaving anger and spitting words. Both had their hands tightly fisted at their sides as if they were struggling to keep them there.

"All these sacrifices, and yet, you'll never get the praise or motherly love you wish to have. Hera will never accept you. Even if you weren't born from my father's indiscretions with other women – and were just a malignant thought that came to be," he bit out. He looked as if he had more words to throw at her but before he could, Athena was lifting a large, cracked boulder over her head.

The rock came down with a heavy bellowing crash, the same one from earlier. The crack in the rock grew and Ares fell to his knees with a roaring groan. He cupped his second hand against the other side of his head as golden ichor began to pour out.

Athena stood over him, unphased by his groaning. "You're hubris is the exact reason he comes to me for insight on the mortal wars and why you are *consistently* excluded from such conversations." The emphasis on the word was harsh and telling. Athena looked up to Demeter, her face softened and her shoulders relaxed.

"I do apologize, Demeter. I did not mean for – for – well, I did not mean to do such things in front of Kore. Please forgive me. If you can see to it that he is cleaned up by tonight, I would be most grateful. I will be collecting him in the morning to take him up to Olympus so he can tell *our* father himself what they all had plotted and carried out." Athena bowed curtly and made her way to her chariot to leave. She gave the reins a good whip that cracked through the field and was off without a second look back.

Demeter spun around to face Kore, her arms rubbing the peplos to warm the child up. "Kore, Dear. What happened? Are you well?" She fussed.

Kore wiped the water from her cheeks as she huddled under the peplos. The little boy's screams rang in her head. But she couldn't tell her mother Aphrodite was near, and with what just transpired between Ares and Athena, Kore felt it wise to keep that bit of information tucked away with the little boy, Adonis.

"I had fallen into the frozen lake, Mama. Did you not hear me calling?" Kore whimpered. Demeter's brows fell, her lips turned down. She pulled Kore into her for a tight hug as tears began to pour out of her eyes.

"Oh, my Daisy. I am so sorry, I did not. I apologize. Please, sit and get warmed up by the fire. I am going to fetch some more poppy to blend down for him. There is a bit in my dark leather trunk by my cot. When you are warmed up please give him some." They both looked to the god moaning and groaning on the ground on the stone in the fetal position as he held his temples and spilled ichor all over.

Kore would have considered it an emergency but her mother seemed rather calm. Allowing her time to warm up before tending to him.

"Will he be alright?" Kore asked softly.

"He will be alright. He has endured worse. You dry and get warm, then tend to him with the milk." Demeter left Kore by the fire to head off. Leaving Kore with the moaning, bleeding God of War. For a moment, she sat and watched him, considering drying off fully or going to get the needed supplies to end his suffering.

She decided on being kind, even if she did not feel he would do the same for anyone else. A heavy sigh left her trembling lips as she lifted from the log, making her way to Ares. He didn't notice her walk up, nor did he notice when she kneeled beside him. But when she took the peplos and dabbed his cheek, he settled.

When most of the ichor was wiped from his face, she assisted him up and helped him to the log. Though he didn't seem the type to accept aid, he did this time, and he did so quietly to Kore's relief. He was rather wobbly on his legs anyway and Kore feared he may be concussed.

"I will grab the bit of milk we have. Then I will clean your wounds for you. Mama went to fetch more poppy, so I assume the amount we have won't be much, but it will be something," she offered sweetly.

As much of a brut Ares was, he was sort of helpless-looking covered in his own ichor, groaning the way he was. Then again, it was a large boulder to crack over someone's head, even for a divine. He nodded softly and held his head between his hands, resting his elbows on his knees.

She left him with the peplos as she stepped into the fort. The dark leather trunk sat unbothered at the foot of Demeter's cot. On her way over to it, she snatched the few rags that sat on the table in the middle of the floor. Flipping the trunk lid open, she dug through the jars as they clanked about with every jostle.

The jar of poppy milk was easily spotted with the thick white cream, nearly gone as her mother had mentioned but the little remaining should be enough to, at the very least, dull the aches Ares was having.

Kore grabbed the milk and a jar of skullcap mixed with yarrow powder. The poultice of powdered herb should help to slow the spill of ichor after cleaning. She collected the jars in her arm with the rags and headed out. The only thing she needed was a bucket of fresh water, luckily Demeter always kept a full one beside the fort entrance.

With everything in hand, Kore took the spot at Ares's side and handed him the milk, "Drink that."

The god did as requested, shooting back the milk with a pinched expression. Kore wet a rag and turned to begin wiping the flaking ichor free from his temple. She tried not to think about who she was helping, it felt too intimate to be so close with him.

There was one god she wouldn't mind this closeness with. One she would happily tend to. She had always found Aidoneus to be handsome, a gorgeous man if she had ever seen one. She knew she had a slight infatuation with him. But the Goddess of Love made it seem like it was more and it gave her something to think about.

Kore continued wiping away ichor off Ares, moving from his cleared cheek to his temple. She had to reach up to brush his hair from the wound and dab it clear. A bit more difficult to reach with his bulging shoulder in the way. With a slight shift to the left and an uncomfortable shift to the right, she tried to find a decent way to reach without pressing her entire body against him.

"Here," he grunted, lowering himself to the ground. He leaned his back against the log and rested his ichor-stained head on her lap. Though this did make it easier, she would have rather struggled to reach.

Now it was entirely too intimate and her robes were

going to be soaked and stained in his ichor. She bit back the slight annoyance and continued cleaning his wounds. Tearing a dry rag in two, Kore placed the powdered herb mix in the center of the cloth. She dribbled enough water into it to create a thick paste and then placed it over the wound with a loose wrapping. His groaning and moaning had turned down just a bit but not by much.

When that was done, Ares turned over for her to repeat the process on the second wound. Which by the looks of it, was far worse than the first as ichor continued to gush from it.

She was clearing off his cheek from the gold stain when her mother returned. With wide eyes, she got to work pulling the milk from the several poppy pods she had plucked. Kore fought with his sticky, gold-coated hair as she searched for the hole of the wound. It wasn't deep but long, traveling from his temple to the top of his head. When she had parted his strands out of the way, her mother had come to their side with the milk.

"Drink this, Ares. It should silence the sting, and your groans of pain."

He snatched the bottle with a relieved sigh and chugged it all down.

"Mama, I think we will need more of the skullcap and yarrow powder. This wound is a bit longer than the last," Kore explained.

Her hands were coated with gold and her dress stained along her lap and still, more ichor poured free. She dabbed and dabbed it away, splashed it with water to rinse, and dabbed some more. His groaning had finally come to a stop at the work of the milk and his head lolled in her lap freely.

His shoulders shook with a chuckle of unknown humor. "Athena believes herself to be so spectacular," he slurred. Kore looked up to Demeter in confusion, and her mother just shrugged with a roll of her eyes. A silent communication that he was about to spew random nonsense once again.

"All because she came from my father's head. Can you believe that? She would not have been there if it were not for the prophecy that worked my father up so harshly. He had lost his senses to it, eating Metis to ensure a child was not born. But one was," his words slurred together in an almost indistinguishable way.

"One child or two. One child or two," he repeated with a soft chuckle. "Maybe two. I wonder where that one may be."

Kore looked back to Demeter who was eyeing Ares with a lifted brow.

"There was only one child that came from your father's head. You can rest assure," Demeter huffed. It wasn't the first time he had mumbled nonsense about two children from Zeus – which was hard to even decipher any other way because Zeus had many children and not all of them were in the traditional sense.

"One boy, one girl. Two boys, Two girls. Girl. Girl. Girl," he chuckled drunkenly again. Kore finished the poultice and placed it over his gash.

"All done," she pushed briskly as she lifted his head to set herself free. She stepped to her mother's side as they looked over the god, now intoxicated by the milk and free of pain.

"He will be out here mumbling his incoherent babblings for a while. Let us get you cleaned up and in bed. My poor child, you must have had such a fright. I am sorry I had not heard your cries." They turned to the fort, leaving Ares alone by the fire to heal or whatever he wanted to do. He could find his way to his sleeping cot.

"It is alright, Mama. I wasn't in the water long, there was a fallen log I grabbed onto."

"What were you doing, sweet child?" Demeter asked as they stepped into their fort.

Kore thought for a moment, she hadn't devised a proper excuse for why or how she fell in.

"Uh – I did not realize I was standing on ice until it was too late," she offered the lie that looked to register with her mother. Demeter sucked in a shallow breath as she thought on the explanation.

"Well, I am overjoyed you are well. But after that, I would prefer you stay in shouting distance from now on.

Understood?"

Kore's shoulders fell, "Yes, Mama."

Back to being a prisoner.

CHAPTER XV

WORD FROM OLYMPUS

With the start of Spring only a few days away, and after the spill in the frozen pond, Demeter was sure to keep Kore close and in view. It was clear she put off many of her own workings to keep near Kore, as to not bother the child with the abrasiveness of Ares. But in the few times Demeter could not keep Kore within view, she reluctantly sent Ares to keep watch.

The hovering left Kore with absolutely no time of her own aside from bathing. But this day seemed to be a bit different than the last few weeks. Ares had left for Olympus to have a word with his father before the sun graced the sky.

With the worry of having to move on to their next destination, Demeter busied herself with gathering their things, double and triple-checking her work, and parting ways with the trees she had tasked with monitoring the fields.

Kore, on the other hand, spent the morning over the once

barren patch. Her vines twisted at her side, a bit fuller than they used to be, but also staying beside her at a reasonable length. They mixed the soil until it was loose and ready while Kore summoned a crocus flower in her palms. A clone she had been waiting to place.

With her palms together, the vines twisted about them to aid in the creation. The golden glow warmed Kore's hands as she pushed the energy through, it intensified as the sprout formed, brighter and brighter until finally fading away to leave a coolness in its place.

Slowly opening her hands, Kore peaked at the newly crafted floret. Full and vibrant with a firm stem and beautiful sprawl of roots. A vine slipped from Kore's wrist to dimple the soil between the tree's roots. Tucked near its trunk for shelter and shade from the harsh sun.

Kore gently placed the flower in its new home and patted the dirt at its base. "There you are, new friend. You will find you have the friendliest of neighbors to aid you." She smiled down at the crocus, its leaves fluttering in thanks. It gave her more than hope, it provided security, though the flower itself would never know.

The vines twisted happily in her robes, joyous to be at her side once more and praising her work as they often did. It wasn't simply because they had missed her or were upset and angry with her for her distance. They needed her as much as she needed them. They didn't have a mind of their own as she once considered, they never had. She was their mind, their body, and their lifeline. Without her care and acknowledgment, they were lifeless.

Demeter had been correct when she said their emotions affected their work, Kore just never considered it included the vines. She grazed her fingers over the top of one of the leathery tendrils at her side, the all-consuming comfort filled her with a sense of peace and tranquility she hadn't felt in many moons.

She sat with them for moments more, watching the crocus as it flourished. The last flower she had replanted in the patch had dwindled over a few short moments, but this one seemed to have taken well to its new home. When Kore was sure the flower was set for her departure, she whispered her farewells as she climbed to her feet.

After dusting her hands off from the sticky, moist soil, she gave a final wave to the flower and the trees before heading back to assist her mother in preparation for the next move.

By the time she had returned to their fort, Hermes was arriving in his gold and white chariot with a bright beaming smile.

"Hermes!" Kore cheered with a face-splitting grin. It had been a few winters since she had seen her favorite brother and she had needed his brightly lit cheeks and helpful words a magnitude of times.

She ran to him with open arms and locked them around his neck upon connection. "I have missed you!"

"As I have missed you, little sister!" He chuckled, embracing her just the same. He spun her around once before setting her down. "Well, you are not so little anymore. I no longer have to look down to talk to you."

"What brings you all this way, Hermes?" Demeter asked. He broke away from Kore and cleared his throat.

"Zeus has requested your return to Olympus. Something about what Ares has been discussing with him, and they have reached a settlement on the matter. You both are to come and hear it as well," he informed with a bit more seriousness to his tone.

Demeter nodded and looked to their fort, "Should we gather our things or will we be returning?"

Hermes looked over the camp around him with a twisted curve to his lip in consideration. "Your collection has grown. I think it would be best to keep it here for now."

Demeter and Kore nodded and stepped onto the golden chariot.

When Ares had left, he wasn't clear on what he wanted to speak with Zeus about. The last time they were called up to Olympus it was to be told they needed to revisit fields they had once mended. And after the incident with Athena and Ares, Kore feared his meddling caused an uproar that would have them circling back again.

As she did before, Kore took the spot between her mother and Hermes. With him, she enjoyed standing and watching the travel, whereas with Ares, Kore preferred to be as far from him as the chariot would allow. Hermes also moved much quicker than Ares and the mortal pace he took.

They arrived at the Golden Bridge just as the sun met its highest point. A speedy and smooth travel that didn't leave Kore's bottom sore. But that didn't keep her heart from speeding up the closer they came to the palace. Her mouth grew dry at the thought of having to return to the fields a third time. It had already been three winters and she was well ready to return to her meadow. She had so much to share with Lotus, and the cypress trees she could hardly contain it.

The chariot came to a steady halt by the stables where Hermes gleefully hopped off to tie them down. Demeter gracefully exited and waited for Kore to do the same.

"I think I would prefer to stay with Hermes for this announcement, Mama. If that is alright. I would rather hear the dreadful words from you," she whispered.

"If Kore wants to stay behind, I do not mind staying with her," Hermes popped from beside them. Demeter looked over her daughter, a gleam of understanding glossed her eyes as she gave a slight bow.

Kore hugged her mother and watched as she entered the great palace. Waiting until she was well out of view and hearing range before speaking.

"What has Ares requested?" she asked, keeping her eyes on the entrance.

Hermes released a giggle, "To aid the mortals in the war. But as I am sure you know, Athena already told Zeus about his and the other's involvement with the Trojans. Of course, that did not go over well with Zeus. He plans to punish the lot of them."

Kore's heart sunk to the pit of her stomach. Punishing Ares would mean he would be excluded from his most favored thing. War. Which meant they would be stuck with him for that much longer.

"Do not look so glum, little sister," Hermes pipped, noticing Kore's change in demeanor. "He says it will bring an end to this war and put Ares in the place he needs him in. I am sure you and your mother will not be affected by it."

Kore hadn't a clue what Hermes meant by that. But if whatever it was Zeus planned brought an end to the war, that hopefully meant her and her mother's return to the meadow.

There were other questions she had for him, ones that burned her tongue with a fierce nature.

How is Aidoneus? She wanted to ask. Hermes was the only one who knew of her admiration for the god, but she hoped her apparent adoration wasn't as clear to him as it was to Aphrodite.

As if to read her thoughts, Hermes perked up from behind the chargers with a devilish grin. "You know, sweet sister, if there is a question you wish to ask, you may ask it."

Warmth lit her cheeks and she ducked her head from him, allowing her hair to shield the flush of gold. "I haven't any questions, Hermes."

"Hm, if you say so. I just assumed you were curious as to what Pita was up to. Silly little hound, he is," he continued to tease. Kore did enjoy the company of the sweet creature.

"Oh, I suppose I was wondering how he was. The hound, of course. Does he miss me terribly?" she teased back.

"Frightfully so."

Kore giggled and tilted her head up to face him, a bit more confident in asking her true questions. "And what of his master? Aidoncus, how is he?"

Hermes held the smile as he cleared his throat, a bit of seriousness fitted him. "He is just the same dark bore he always is. Busy judging the extra shades spilling in from this war."

A hard rock formed in Kore's stomach at his words. She knew a few of those shades were sent by her vines and she wondered if Aidoneus would know that was their cause to an end. Vines cast out by a little-known divine. She ducked her face again, gripping the crystal at her neck for security.

"Hopefully it will all end soon. Then you and your mother can return home and Demeter can return to making her delicious honey bread. Hestia has been in charge of it, and thus far, I am not impressed."

Kore couldn't help but let out the erupting laughter that came from her. Hermes was never shy about his dislike for Hestia's bread. Kore never found any fault in it, perhaps her honey bread was not as sweet as Demeter's, but that did not mean it was not as tasty.

"I can imagine it will be the second thing she does, right after checking her bees for honey," Kore laughed.

The sound of the palace doors groaned open to present Demeter and no Ares. The smile that had burned Kore's cheeks instantly fell, ready for the discouraging news to be shared. What other reason would Ares stay behind but to be given more orders on where to take them next? Her mother stepped to them with a hard scowl pressing her lips.

"Will we be staying in the fields?" Kore asked grimly. Demeter looked confused for a moment before a smile spread her pointed expression.

"Not at all. We may return to our meadow, my Daisy," Demeter said with tear-filled eyes. News that seemed too good to be true. After so long of hoping to hear the words, she couldn't believe they were finally free. Kore could hardly contain her excitement as she jumped into a tight embrace with her mother. Hermes and his sweet warmth joined in with a joyous cheer. Not truly understanding their struggles, but happy to be there nonetheless.

They still needed to retrieve their trunks from camp and it appeared that Ares was to stay on Olympus a bit longer. Breaking away from the embrace of her mother, Kore hopped onto the chariot. Ready to be on their way and return to the meadow she had missed so dearly.

"We only need to gather our things," Demeter added in a cheery tune.

"No worries. I will take you back to Thouria to collect your things, and then off to your meadow," Hermes beamed, guiding Kore onto the chariot.

    Warmth flooded her chest, filling her cheeks with a golden hue. They were returning to the meadow. To their chickens and goats and peace. To Lotus, Morea, Syke, and Ampelos.

    They were finally returning home. And Kore would be returning with a bit more understanding in her powers and vines.

ABOUT THE AUTHOR

    Ambrosia spends most of her days at home. When she is not writing out fantasies, she can be found homeschooling three highly rambunctious kids or tending to the three pets that also call her 'mom'.
    To add to her list of things to do with herself, she also studies herbalism and practices in the craft, which she has incorporated her knowledge of such topics throughout her works.
    Most often Ambrosia spends time relaxing by sipping tea and watching horror movies.

OTHER WORKS BY AMBROSIA

The Taking of Persephone Series:
Kore
Hades
Demeter

    From the fans of Rachel Smythe's Lore Olympus webtoons graphic novel and Madeline Miller's Circe and Songs of Achilles, mythology, fantasy, historical fiction, and romance will enjoy this classic retelling in this four-part series.

    Before Persephone was known as The Dread Queen, she was but a young goddess who went by the name of Kore, pulling flowers from soil to create life. Nothing more is spoken on the all feared Queen and her rise to power.

    Not of her journey. Not of her time in the realm of the dead where she showed the King of Darkness what it means to be loved.

    Experience the full story from all three perspectives to see how things panned out for each of them and what really happened to Demeter during Kore's time with Hades. The first three books of this series trace back through Kore's childhood, Demeter's struggles, and Hades betrayal - all leading up to the next chapter of this series, Persephone (book 4).

The Dark Realms Series:
Sunflower in the Shadows

"Hi, I'm Mina Karim and I'm... Well, I'm not too sure what I am. Not anymore anyway. But what I am sure of, is never, under any circumstances, offer your soul to a demon while drunk."

After breaking every rule in the book, Mina and her friends accidentally summon an ambivalent demon, creating a domino effect of terrors they now must find a way to fix.

The problem? Nobody truly knows about the power they stumbled upon. Now, Mina finds herself working with the very demon who took her soul, to find a way to break their tether. Will they be able to break the bond? Or will the truth send them spiraling further into the endless depths of the Six Circles?

Demons and Mortals Series:
Best-Seller
Muse
Revenge
Demon King

Some mortals make deals with demons for riches or fame, but the women of the Comeaux family want none of those.

A short series of interconnecting stand-alones about three mortal sisters who want the best out of their careers, and three demon brothers they were promised to. Each story is four chapters long, so they are perfect for a quick, spicy palate cleanser.

Printed in Dunstable, United Kingdom